SCHOOL FOR APES

Words Matter Publishing
P.O. Box 531
Salem, Il 62881
www.wordsmatterpublishing.com

ISBN 13: 978-1-947072-95-4
ISBN 10: 1-947072-95-1

Library of Congress Catalog Card Number: 2018956432

For my wonderful family

My beautiful wife, Mary

My daughters; Laura, Peri, Kiara and Tegan

And my grandchildren; Ivy and River

ACKNOWLEDGEMENTS

It doesn't take one person to write a book, well it does, but not without help and support.

Firstly, I must thank my long-suffering wife Mary who has had to endure endless talks about apes and monkeys and had our kitchen covered with various photographs and books covering primates and their habitats.

Secondly my children, Laura, Peri, Kiara and Tegan who without their enthusiasm and input, this book may never have happened . . . and yes Kiara did find herself turned into a baboon for literary purposes! My third thank you has to go out to my parents. My recently departed mother's love of books lighted my fire years ago and both her and my father's support through the years have driven me to this point. Harry and Alice Todd, Paul and Sharon Callaghan and other various aunts, uncles and cousins who have supported me, not just with this book but with others.

A massive thank you to friends and colleagues who have offered support and have had listen to me endlessly talking about monkeys: Julie, Barrie, Tracey, Shehmina, Mandie, Lee, Jason, Jamie C, Caroline, Norman, Jamie G, Dillon, Steve, Graham, Chris and Robert. All of whom I have probably bored senseless with plot devices and ideas, and of course Scott who's kind words gave me the push I needed to continue.

I would like to thank Tammy Koelling and her hard working team at

Wordsmatterpublishing for believing in me and my work and giving an unknown author the chance to shine.

Finally, I would like to thank you the reader. For without you, I wouldn't be writing this now. You've picked up this book by an author you probably haven't heard of before and spent your hard earned money in buying this title. I hope your faith is justified. . .

All our lives are a story. Just make sure yours is a good one.

FOREWORD

Every story must start with a step. This was mine. I always loved to write, ever since I was young. I would write for my parents. Everything from stories to poems... I had dreams. Then, life happened. A family, a mortgage, bills, work. Despite all of this, I never stopped dreaming. I still wrote for my daughters. Tales of German Shepard's, how the flamingo became pink and tales from history; Life continued and past, and my children grew into beautiful young ladies, and still my dream continued. But, every dream must come to an end and it would be in 2015 that I decided my dream needed to stop just being a dream and start becoming a reality. I always believed that everyone has a story to tell, but not everyone has the time to be able to tell that story.

School for Apes happened by accident. We had decided to take the family to the city of Nottingham for the weekend. I wanted to see the caves, the castle and the galleries of justice, so off we went. And, I have to say it is a lovely city and would recommend a visit. It was on our second night in the city that the idea for School for Apes became a reality. Every story needs a beginning, every story needs an idea and at the time I was working on a series of short stories for a Doctor Who book. The day had been hectic, but well worth it and after an enjoyable evening with my family we kicked back and chilled before going to bed.

It was at three in the morning when I was woken by a dream. With my head spinning I ran into the bathroom and began making notes while kneeling on the cold, hard floor. With a smile on my face and ideas in my head, I turned off the light and sneaked back into bed. When I woke in the morning I was confronted by a series of notes scattered over the bathroom floor. Little pieces of paper, which I had no answer for. Each one had a single word or phrase. Hazeldene. . .Olivia. . .Monkey. . .Dominic. . .School for Apes. It was my writing, but I had no idea why I had written the words. Throughout the day we visited Nottingham's Galleries of Justice, then a lovely family meal. But, throughout I was perturbed by the words and bit by bit, my dream came to me.

I was standing with a series of people holding a book in my hands. The title was written in chalk and sprawled across the book. Was this a sign? Was it a premonition? Who knows...? I had the title, all I needed was a story...so here it is and I hope you enjoy it.

Chapter 1
DOMINIC

"Dominic Atwell!"
The cry of a voice rang out through the classroom and Dominic winched at the sound, knowing his name at this volume was never a good sign. He sat close to the window and spent most of his school day gazing out through the blinds at the lush green grass of the field beyond the confines of the class. Although, today the grass was looking a dull brown in colour and a group of adults was congregating around a large area where the lavish green of the field met the dead area of grass. He lowered his head close to his wooden desk in an attempt to disappear and tried to hide the smirk that was slowly sneaking its way across his face. "Dominic Atwell!" the voice sounded crosser than ever as it ran over the heads of the other pupils in the class. "I am talking to you!"

"No, you're not..." Dominic whispered under his breath. "You're shouting," he grinned heartily as he spoke to himself. He looked at the desk by his and smirked as the boy next to him stifled a laugh as the teacher surged through the rows of tables to his position at the back of the class.

"You're in for it now Dom," whispered the boy under his

1

breath, then cast his gaze away from the red-faced teacher bearing down on him.

"What did you say?" the voice raged, filling the air around him. Dominic looked up from his desk and for the first time gazed into the face of his teacher. She stood over him, staring down from her elevated position, and rested her hands on the front of his desk. Dominic stared into her bloodshot eyes as they filled with anger, then at her flaring nostrils as they thrust in and out as she blew air out through her nose. The vein on her temple pumped viciously as her blood pressure rose. Dominic watched, convinced that it was about to burst at any moment.

He smiled innocently at her. "Nothing Miss," he said in his softest, sweetest voice.

"Don't you dare lie to me Dominic Atwell!" she stormed. "I know you said something...just like I know you had something to do with that." She pointed out of the window toward the patch of dead grass in the center of the field.

"Me?" Dominic asked astonished, following her finger and staring out of the window as though he had noticed the field out-side the school for the first time.

"Don't you give me that!" she snapped, elevating each word with a slight pause.

"You can't think I had anything to do with that..." Dominic said, placing his hands on his chest and mocking innocence.

"I don't think Mr. Atwell, I know." She leant close to Dominic, and he stared at her as she breathed with anger before him. She was in her mid-forties and quite attractive for her age, consider-ing. Her face was lined around her eyes, and there were traces of bags beneath her glasses. Her neat brown hair was tied tightly in a bun and sat perched on the top of her head, while a pair of small rimmed spectacles sat on the end of her nose. Her face was so close to Dominic's that he could almost count the freckles which

2

covered her face and Dominic smiled to himself as they reminded him of a bowl of Rice Krispies battling through layers of milk. "I know, and so does Mr. Reed." Dominic blinked as he realised that she had still been talking this whole time while he was staring at her. "His office now!" she snapped and pointed toward the front of the class where the door stood closed barring the corridor from the classroom.

"Fine," he grunted and pushed his chair back, forcing it closer to the wall, letting it slide across the floor scraping the wooden surface. "I know the way," he murmured as he picked his way through the rows of tables, with dozens of accusing eyes staring and watching his slow progress through the classroom. Dominic reached the door and paused with his hand on the handle and looked back at his classmates, his smile fading to regret as he saw the pity in the faces of the pupils at their desks. Then his eyes wandered over to the accusing glare of his teacher, who still stood by his desk, arms folded over her chest and a look of...disappointment, more than anger crossing her face. He sighed and pushed open the door and slid into the empty, lonely corridor and gazed along its cold walls.

"Sorry about that children," he could hear the voice from inside apologise. "Now that this little disruption has left...we shall continue where we left off...Julie...please."

Dominic sighed and leant for a moment with his back pressed firmly against the wall of the corridor and listened as the girl's voice continued reading from a passage of the book that they had been studying before the incident.

"Again, Dominic?" the male voice was soft in tone. Dominic looked around from his silent vigil and looked in the direction of the school caretaker.

"Yes," he nodded sadly and pushed his back from the wall.

"When will it stop, son?" called the caretaker as Dominic passed him and sulked away down the hall. "You act like a monkey

3

lad...and they'll treat you like one!"

Dominic paid him no attention, but nevertheless, his words rang true in his mind, "act like a monkey...they'll treat you like a monkey." He kept turning the words over and over as he walked slowly along the corridor toward the room at the other end of the school. Part of his mind couldn't understand why he kept doing bad things, while another reveled in the attention that he got, good or bad. The walls of the school watched him as he walked down the corridor, seemingly gazing down with their own silent accusation. For every poster and every painting decorating the wall, a pair of baleful eyes stared down from their mounted position. The simple plain wooden door of the headmaster's office loomed at the end of the corridor and beckoned him forward...ever nearer, ever closer. The silence of the corridor was beaten back by the sound of his own breathing, and the relentless thump...thump... thump of his heartbeat echoed in his ears. He paused outside the door and glanced up at the wooden obstacle, his hand hovering over the wood, and he strained to listen to the voices which crept beneath the door. He could hear muffled words being spoken, but couldn't make out the meaning or who was speaking and slowly his hand raised and curled as he attempted to knock. He glanced through the window by the office and caught the sad gaze from the school receptionist. She quickly reverted her eyes back to a large pile of papers which lay on her desk. He sighed and rested his head against the door, then against his own will brought his hand down against the wood, his knock echoing through the corridor three times, matching the sound of his own heartbeat.

"Come..." the voice from the other side of the door was clear. Sighing heavily, he pushed at the handle and sunk as he entered the room. The office was large, and held two long wooden desks, the first holding a computer system with a monitor resting on the surface of the table. A steaming cup sat close to the keyboard and

Dominic was drawn to the wisp of vapour as it rose from the steaming brown liquid within the ceramic cup. The other table was strewn with sheaves of paper, masked with figures and diagrams and official documents as they battled for attention amongst the debris of pens and pencils. Small potted plants scattered the office, leaning on window sills, tables and cabinets while larger pots sat on the floor decorating the office. Two gentlemen sat in large leather swivel chairs, one Dominic recognised, the other was a stranger to him. His headmaster wore a stern expression to match his stern brown suit and plain white shirt. His black hair was neat and tidy and copied the flow of his trimmed facial hair, and as Dominic entered the room, he stroked his moustache as though smoothing down an imaginary hair. "Dominic..." he said and looked at the other man opposite him.

The other man was considerably older and in contrast to the prim and smart suit that the headmaster wore, his clothing was untidy, his blue shirt bore an open top button, and his black tie was hanging limply from the collar falling slightly over a rounding stomach, bending to the contours of the man's body. His grey suit looked too small for his ample frame as both the legs and the arms of the jacket and trousers rode up his body exposing his shirt and white socks. His hair grew at intermittent patches on the side of his head, and the sun shone off the balding area at the top of his temple and stretched across the back of his cranium. The older man never smiled as Dominic walked in, simply beckoned him forward, then pointed to a low-level fabric sofa which sat partially hidden behind the door. Dominic felt his heart sink further as he turned and faced the frowning faces of both his mother and father as they sat huddled together on the reclining furniture.

"Mr. and Mrs. Atwell...Dominic," started the older man as he looked toward the family as Dominic took his place between his parents.

"Can we ask what this is about?" asked Dominic's father in a stern voice, glancing down at his son and frowning angrily at the boy.

"Certainly," stated the older man. "As you know Dominic has been...how shall I put it..." he searched for the word for a moment then smiled at Dominic. "A challenge," he finally said. He turned in his chair and spoke to the headmaster, "Mr. Reed...if you could be so kind?"

The headmaster nodded and rose from his seat and walked over the room to a large metal cabinet and opened the top drawer, pulling a large file from the confines of the interior. "Who are you?" demanded Mr. Atwell as the headmaster handed over the file to the older man.

"Oh, I beg your pardon," said the man in mock surprise. "Didn't I introduce myself?" he smiled as Mr. Atwell shook his head. "My name is Mr. Andrews...and I am the coordinator for the local schools in the area. You might say I'm the governor," his teeth flashed as he opened the file resting in his hands and he allowed his eyes to drift over the words. "You see Mr...Mrs. Atwell, Dominic here is my problem."

"That's a bit harsh," said Mrs. Atwell, placing an arm around her son defensively.

"Hardly..." purred Mr. Andrews. "You see, I've worked across the area and in every school I 've been in there's been one word which has plagued me...one word which has disrupted the entire phase of that school..." he looked straight at the cowering figure between the two adults. "Dominic," he whispered and leant forward close to the boy.

"How dare you!" snapped Mr. Atwell.

"How dare I!" snapped Mr. Andrews. "How dare I!" he laughed and threw the heavy file on the top of the table, shaking the contents under the sudden pressure of the excessive weight.

"Every school, Mr. Atwell...every school," he turned to the window and gazed out as if speaking to the trees which lined the pavement outside the room. "There have been so many cases involving your child...from truancy to vandalism."

"Vandalism?"

"Yes...Mr. Atwell, as well you know," he turned back and smiled. "How many times has your checkbook been forced to pay for damages caused by your son?" he asked. "How many broken tables...chairs...windows?" his voice trailed off as he gazed back out of the window. "Then there's the graffiti..."

"That hasn't been proved," interrupted Mrs. Atwell.

"He's signed his work!" snapped Mr. Andrews, laughing and turning back to them. "Then there is the constant cheek in the classroom. The disrespect for the teachers...the bullying," he shook his head and looked at Dominic. "I am sorry Mr...Mrs. Atwell, but your child is a disruptive influence in the classroom."

"I refute that!" stormed Mr. Atwell. "My son is special," he looked at his son and smiled slightly as he spoke, but even through the false smile flashed toward Dominic, the boy could see a sadness hidden within his gaze. "He needs special attention, that's all. It's not him that's failing sir, but your education system."

Mr. Andrews sighed, removing his glasses from his face, rubbing the bridge of his nose. Pinching the skin between his fingers, he spoke slowly, "Please, Mr. Atwell. You have to understand that your son has been given every opportunity and time and time again he has shown himself to be a destabilizing influence over the rest of the classroom."

"In your opinion," countered Mr. Atwell.

"Very well," said Mr. Andrews sighing. He walked slowly to the old wooden desk before the window, and bending over, he pulled open the bottom drawer and removed a large bulging folder. He turned to Mr. Atwell and dropped the heavy file on the desk before him. He perched himself on the edge of the table and opened the paper binding of the folder and stared at the top few pages, flicking over the words which stared out of the paper. He began to speak slowly and deliberately. "Over the last few years Mr. Atwell, your child has attended every school in the local area...and all with the same results," he scanned the pages of the folder sadly as he spoke. "Dominic is a disruptive child who has no intention of learning," he quoted, then turned to another page. "Dominic has a low attention span and will never amount to much unless he changes his attitude toward learning..." Another page, "Dominic has spent more time this term in detention than in lessons...this boy has no intention of following the curriculum and has more interest in disturbing his fellow pupils." He looked at Mr. Atwell, "the list goes on and on sir."

"I don't believe half the things that are being said about my son," interrupted Mrs. Atwell. "He's a good boy...really," the lie spoken stood out strongly, and the desperation in Mrs. Atwell's words belied her own conviction.

Again Mr. Andrews sighed and read from the folder. Picking pages at random, he began reading from one page to another. "Dominic was fighting...running through the girls changing room naked...salt in the teachers coffee...bringing foreign objects into school...swearing...placing cling-film over the toilets...sugar in the caretakers fuel tank...truancy...locking a girl in the boys toilets... water bombing the governors car...rude snowmen...worms in a teachers desk...altering test papers...turning up the temperature in an egg incubator...releasing frogs into a nursery...pins on seats...the list goes on and on," sighed Mr. Andrews as he flicked from page to page. "Shall I continue?" he asked, shaking his head and pushing his glasses down his nose as he looked at Dominic's parents. The headmaster of the school turned and looked out of the window, unable to meet their glare, watching as various people collected pieces of damaged grass from the field beyond the office. "When I first became a teacher many years ago, Mr. Atwell, I had a dream... no, a vision, that every child had a bright future. Every child would learn under my tutelage and grow to become great men and brilliant women. He looked straight at Dominic, "But in all my years of teaching I have never met any child who has refused constant education and has remained persistent with this unruly behaviour." Mr. Andrews looked down sadly at his shoes as he spoke his final words, "I am sorry to say this, and I have never had the misfortune to admit that in all my years of schooling...your child is...in my opinion...unteachable."

Chapter 2
HAZELDENE

A sharp, sudden knock at the door alerted Miss Olivia Hawthorne to the presence of a stranger on the other side of the entrance. She looked up from her desk and called over to the closed wooden structure barring her office from the outside world. "Come!" she called sternly.

The door opened very slightly at first, and a small ferrety man poked his head around the wooden barrier to her office. "Miss Hawthorne," he stammered, almost apologetic in his nature.

"Ah, Mr. Swinehurst...please come in," she purred as she looked at the bloated features of the face at the door. She watched as the small man pushed his way into the room and walked slowly across the floor, his eyes darting around the confines of the office as he strode confidently toward the plush leather chairs by the ornate wooden table. Miss Hawthorne rose from her seat to greet the man as he moved across the floor of her office. She realised as she stood over his rotund body that she towered over him. He measured at just over four feet in height, and his neat, black suit struggled to match his frame, with the arms and legs bulging and riding up his limbs, exposing his white socks and blue shirt beneath the heavy material of his suit. She beckoned toward the seat on the opposite side of the table, indicating for him to sit. Mr. Swinehurst stared at the seat for a moment, as though the chair had suddenly grown teeth and was about to devour him like the chicken sandwich he had himself devoured on the train ride to this place. A vast, thick globule of white mayonnaise rode his red tie as it crossed his swelling stomach. Mr. Swinehurst reached out for the chair, pulling it backward over the floor and making a harsh scraping noise as the furniture dragged over the wooden flooring. "And for what do I have the pleasure of your company?" cooed Miss Hawthorne sweetly, flashing him a sincere smile and holding out her long spindly hand for him to shake.

"You know perfectly well the purpose of my visit, Miss Hawthorne," said the measly little man. His face bulged as he spoke and Miss Hawthorne watched as his skin turned a subtle crimson in colour as his eyes widened and swelled through his thick-rimmed spectacles. He puffed his cheeks out and removed his bowler hat from his head and placed it on the table before him, breathing in heavily as though he had just run a marathon. The exertion of walking from the door to the table had apparently tired him and small pearls of sweat formed around his greasy, black, untidy hair. He looked at her hand for a moment before accepting it. Planting his thick sweaty lips on the back of her hand, he then lowered himself into the seat and pulled it close to the desk. "Now Miss Hawthorne...I suggest we get down to business."

"Quite," agreed Miss Hawthorne, as she placed her hands before her and sat prim and tall in her chair on the other side of the desk. "Refreshments?"

"That is very kind of you..." purred Mr. Swinehurst, smiling through his thin lips which bulged and spread across his swollen piggy cheeks. "But I really think we should get straight to business." He leant to one side and pulled a large black briefcase onto his lap and stabbed at the lock on the edge of the case. The hinges of the case swung open, popping the lid, and the small man's head disappeared inside the case as he rummaged around the contents of the bag. Miss Hawthorne could hear papers mixing with the variety of pens and pencils as they moved around the bottom of the briefcase. He smiled as he removed from the case a small bundle of paper tied neatly by a large blue ribbon and placed it carefully on the desk by the case.

"Nonsense, Mr. Swinehurst," smiled Miss Hawthorne pleasantly as she spoke. "There is always time for tea." She reached across the desk and grasped at a small silver bell which sat on the edge of the table. The bell made a gentle noise as it rang out across the room and the slight chime was greeted by a gruff voice on the other side of an adjacent door.

"My Lady..." came the voice through the wooden barrier.

"Tea...please Grant," she called, then glanced back to Mr. Swinehurst who was watching her through his thick glasses. "Now then...where were we?" she asked.

"We were about to start," he replied curtly and tugged at the ribbon, allowing the strands to fall over the desk.

"That's right," Miss Hawthorne agreed nodding. "Right then, what seems to be the matter?" she asked innocently.

"Miss Hawthorne, for several years the school has been running at a loss of revenue and since going through the accounts for the last year, I am saddened to inform you that unless the school gets a sizeable increase in funds for this year the bank will have no other option than to close down the academy once and for all." The small man wheezed as he uttered this long sentence. He slammed the lid of the case closed firmly and took off his glasses and stared at her. "I am sorry Miss Hawthorne, but I am forced to announce that as of the end of this academic year...unless you can procure additional funding from elsewhere...Hazeldene will be closing for the final time." He stood and pushed the wad of papers across the desk in her direction, "I think you will find all of this in order...I suggest you read it, Miss Hawthorne." He rose and collected his hat from the table and nodded in her direction. "I am sorry, but my business here is done. I can see my own way out," he said humbly.

The handle of the door at the side of the office twitched under the pressure from the other side, and Miss Hawthorne was briefly distracted from the small man scurrying across the floor. "But Mr. Swinehurst!" she called as her guest pulled at the main door and let himself out of her office. She watched him hurry along the hallway, his stumpy little legs carrying him further and further away from her office. "Your tea," she said softly, her voice sadly trailing off into a whisper as the door opened to the side of her. She looked at the widening crack of the door and sighed heavily, walking over to the window. "Just be a darling and place it on the desk, would you?" she asked over her shoulder. She listened as the heavy footsteps of her butler thudded against the floor, and the slight clink of the porcelain cups nudged each other on the silver tray. She folded her arms and stared wistfully over the grounds of the house, watching as the sun began its slow descent over the edge of the distant treetops. "Could you find Mr. Hindle please?" she asked and smiled slightly despite her growing mood. The butler grunted his derision and left the room, closing the door gently behind him as he moved.

She stared over the expanse of the grounds and sighed again, feeling depression sweep over her like a tidal wave of emotion. Alone she could feel the pressure build up around her as the weight of expectation from both governors and parents threatened to consume her. The corners of her mouth slowly fell away, chasing any sign of a smile from her face. She could feel a single tear form in the corner of her eye as she continued to stare over the grounds and she strained to hear the sounds of children from outside her window...but nothing. She cast her eyes to the floor and sniffed removing her glasses and rubbing the bridge of her nose, her eyes clamped tight shut from the world around her.

A slight knock on the door alerted her to the company, and she attempted to regain her posture before the door slowly moved open. A man's face poked through the open gap and smiled into the room. "Where's the parasite?" he smirked as he posed the question, to which he probably could have guessed the answer.

"Mr. Swinehurst? He's gone," Miss Hawthorne answered reluctantly, a slight quiver in her voice hiding the threat of tears. The man moved quietly into the room, looking down at his feet as he walked silently across the floor and to the table. He was in his early forties and neatly dressed in a simple plain black suit adorned with a garish red question mark pin badge sitting proudly on his lapel. A black tie hung around his neck from a tight-fitting white shirt which remained unbuttoned at the collar. He looked at her through large baleful brown eyes and smiled as he reached for the small teapot on the silver tray, his stubble breaking and stretching as his mouth widened from the sudden movement, revealing a row of white teeth.

"Tea...honey?" he enquired glancing from the tray toward the window, where Miss Hawthorne still stood gazing through the clear glass panes. He poured the warm brown liquid into a small cup and pushed it across the desk as she nodded quietly, before pouring a second cup and dropping a spoon of sugar into the depths before adding a splash of milk. He looked at her sadly and added both milk and sugar to her cup and stirred the liquid.

She listened to the clink of the spoon as it echoed around the cup and smiled inwardly at her companion...always looking after her. Although she had never told him, she liked his attention... maybe a little more than she cared to admit. She continued to gaze out of the window as she finally found the courage to speak. "All of this," she indicated out across the grounds and into the distance. "I used to play here as a child," she said wistfully, listening as he placed the cup on the desk and moved around the table until coming to a rest by her side, placing a reassuring hand on her arm. "My father used to take me up there," she said, pointing out over the lawn and into the trees. "He used to say that is our own little adventure world." Tears formed in her eyes as she spoke, "That was before...when I was young."

"Olivia..." whispered Mr. Hindle.

"It's alright," she whispered back through tear stained eyes. "This is my home," she said firmly, turning her head to face him. "It always has been and always will be...no matter what some jumped up little man says." She could feel the frustration rising through her body, and it threatened to overwhelm her emotions.

"Have you read it?" asked Mr. Hindle. "The report?" She followed his eyesight to the desk where the thickly bound leather binder sat on the top of the table and shook her head. "May I?" he asked and waited briefly for her to nod her head allowing him permission to read the pages of the folder. She continued to stare out over the grounds, her body silhouetted in the sunlight and a halo shone over her body as light poured in through the window panes. Mr. Hindle settled in the small leather chair opposite her seat at the desk and glanced up at her, resting his hand on the thick wad of paper and smiled. "You're beautiful," he said softly and grinned as he could see her smiling back through the reflection in the glass.

"You need your eyes examined," she laughed, still staring out of the window.

"There's nothing wrong with my eyesight...and you are...to me." He opened the file and flicked through the paper scanning over the words on the pages.

Miss Hawthorne smiled at his compliment and watched him through the reflective surface of the glass. She cared for him deeply, but even after all the years of working together as colleagues and friends, she still could not find the words to tell him how she felt. "This house...is not my home anymore, it feels more like a prison." She quietly said. She sighed and turned to the table and placed herself in her chair and watched as Mr. Hindle continued to flick through the pages of the document. "How bad is it?" she asked. Mr. Hindle shook his head and continued to flick through the pages. "Eronymous..."

He looked up, smiling through his own sadness, and shook his head, "It's not good Olivia," he said eventually.

"What does it say?" she asked.

"Well...do you want the whole story or the edited highlights?" he asked.

"Tell me the worst."

"That's not going to be hard," he said glancing back into the pages of the folder. "Per these figures, we are officially bankrupt...."

"We can't be, Eronymous...we just can't be!" exclaimed Miss Hawthorne, pinching the bridge of her nose with her slim thin fingers.

"I'm sorry, my Dear," he said softly, rising from his seat and slowly walking behind her chair. He placed his hands gently on her shoulders and softly began massaging her tense muscles. "But unless we can find another source of income...Hazeldene will be forced to close permanently at the end of the year."

Chapter 3
Too Kool for School

The television rang out in the corner of the room, and Dominic sat on the floor glued to the images on the screen as they sprang out in all their colourful glory into the house around him. He watched in awe as figures battled and fought out their lives on the screen, their bodies twisting and contorting as they rose and fell. The colours flashed across his face as he absently reached for the discarded bag of sweets by his hand. The small round sugar filled pellets spilled from the packet as it was dragged across the carpet and raised to Dominic's mouth. He filled his cheeks with the confectionary and chewed absently, frowning as he strained to hear the words of the characters on the screen. The sound of his parent's voices drifted through the house from the kitchen behind the closed door. He briefly glanced toward the stubborn barrier of the kitchen and lowered his head sadly as he heard the arguments he had heard time and time again. Somewhere deep within his mind, he knew he was the cause of the argument, but he also knew he couldn't help the things he did. He sighed with regret and a small part of him wished he could change before that small voice inside him was pushed down deep into the pit of his stomach under the weight of sweets, chocolate, and crisps.

"Well he's not staying at home with me!" snapped Mrs. Atwell as she stood by the sink, her fingers digging tightly on the metallic edge of the basin.

"Well, he certainly can't come to work with me!" roared Mr. Atwell as he countered his wife's argument. "I am a very busy man," he smiled at his own logic.

Mrs. Atwell laughed, "Oh please Reg, you tell other people to do all the work while you sit behind a desk."

"I am a very important person!" he snapped. "It's my business and people rely on me…. I don't have time to babysit…" he paused to find the words to express about his own son, but struggled and simply looked at the door as though gazing through the wood and into the room beyond.

"Go on…say it…the boy," urged Mrs. Atwell.

"Look…" Mr. Atwell said, attempting to pull himself back from his position. "All I'm trying to say is a building site is no place for a young boy." He stood from the small wooden chair at the kitchen table and walked slowly around the furniture to the sink. Placing his hands on his wife's waist, he gazed into her eyes as he turned her around to face him. "He might get hurt," he smiled gently as he spoke. "All those tools…and the language…oh the language, definitely not what we want our son to hear. He would be better off at home with you…his mother. Think of the things you could teach him," Mr. Atwell pulled her close to his chest and held her in his arms as he spoke. "Call it home tutelage."

"I suppose…it could be fun…" she said begrudgingly but sounded unconvinced as her eyes strayed to the window. "First thing in the morning," she said softly as she pulled out of her husband's grip.

Dominic turned in his bed and stared through hazy eyes at the small digital clock which sat on a small set of drawers by his bed. He blinked out the sleep from his eyes and smiled to himself as the illuminating red lights flashed 08:23 at him. He pulled the blankets over his head and closed his eyes and sighed…. "Wednesday morning…and I don't have to get up for school…bliss," he thought. He felt a warm surge run through his body and a slight rumble niggle at his stomach. He swung his feet out from under the warmth of the blankets and placed them on the rubbish-strewn floor of his bedroom. His legs and body followed as he sat upright in bed and listened as he could hear sounds from the radio drift from the kitchen below. He imagined his mother moving about the kitchen, dancing from sink to cooker and back again. He shuffled his feet across the floor of his room kicking aside a combination of pens, toys and empty crisp packets as he crossed to the door. A sudden rush of cold air forced him to pull his striped pyjama top together, and he fumbled for the buttons as he fastened the material. The distraction of the cold chased away the recent gnaw of hunger from his mind as he crossed the carpeted landing toward the bathroom door.

Mrs. Atwell stood in the kitchen, briefly pausing by the sink as she heard the flush of the toilet from upstairs. Her heart sank as she listened to the gentle tread of Dominic's footsteps as he made his way down the stairs and through the hall toward the kitchen. The door swung open, and Dominic stood framed in the doorway dressed in his blue striped pyjamas, the smile fading quickly from his face as he stared aghast at his mother.

Dominic could not believe the sight which greeted him in the kitchen. His mother stood dressed smartly in a prim tight black skirt, which was complemented by a simple white blouse. Her hair was tied back into a ponytail which fell down her back. He gazed around the kitchen and saw no signs of breakfast which he had anticipated, but instead a neat and tidy bare room which was decorated by the back door with a large wooden easel. A wad of paper hung from clips at the top of the board, and he looked back at his mother shaking his head.

"Dominic…" she began. "Hurry up and get your breakfast, you have to get ready for school," she said smiling indicating at the easel by her side.

"Mum!" he whined.

"Now…now…Dominic, your father and I have decided, if you can't attend school then we must provide home tuition."

"But mum…" Dominic groaned.

"But nothing, young man!" she snapped. "You will eat your breakfast, then go and get ready for school. I will expect you to attend by nine o' clock," she checked her watch on her slender wrist. "You have less than half an hour…or else," her voice was tinged with a slight threat, and Dominic winched under the malice in her voice. He sighed and moved to the cupboard, and he pulled down a bowl from inside and reached for the corn flakes which sat at the bottom of the shelf. Placing himself at the table, he poured the cereal into the bowl and reached for the bottle of milk which had been placed for him in the middle of the table. He absently poured the white fluid over the small flakes, watching them float in the bowl. He stared as the milk splashed over his breakfast and spilt onto the top of the table, and his mind wandered to his new 'school.' Home learning, he wondered briefly as he shovelled a large spoonful of cornflakes into his mouth. How bad could it be? Milk fell onto his top as he chewed and his thoughts wandered to his teacher…"I wonder who it is," he thought as he thrust a second spoonful of cereal into his mouth.

Dominic stood outside the kitchen door half an hour later and stared at the obstacle which was standing staring back at him. Behind this was his new teacher…

The door swung open as Dominic pushed his way into the kitchen and he stared at the figure before him and allowed his mouth to fall open in disbelief. "Mum," he whispered.

Mrs. Atwell turned and smiled at her son and shook her head, "no...no...no... for the next few hours, I'm Mrs. Atwell." She laughed and turned her back to him and began to write on the large white pad which hung limply from the wooden easel by the kitchen sink. Dominic stood in shock, unsure what to do as his mother pulled the lid off a thick black marker pen. He watched as she wrote in big letters across the clean page. The ink etched over the paper as she wrote M-R-S. A-T-W-E-L-L in large letters and turned to face her son. "Come on...sit down," she urged waving him into the kitchen. He stepped forward into the room, slowly at first, his eyes scanning the kitchen in case another adult jumped out on him.

His mother watched as Dominic walked slowly into the room. She impatiently glanced at her watch and tapped her foot against the hard, cold floor of the kitchen. She beckoned him to sit at the table and folded her arms frowning at the speed he crossed the floor. As Dominic sat, she smiled and looked around the kitchen and began to speak as though addressing a room full of children. "Good morning class," she spoke clearly, a huge grin spreading across her face as she stifled a reserved laugh. "I am your teacher, Mrs. Atwell," she spread her hands out as she spoke and waved behind her at the easel. Her hand reached to her mouth to cover her obvious delight. Dominic glanced around the room at his phantom classmates and back toward his mother who was obviously enjoying her new role as teacher. "Today we will be studying fractions and square roots," she clapped her hands together as she spoke and frowned as a groan broke the quiet of the kitchen. "Is there a problem, Mr. Atwell?" Dominic frowned and shook his head. "I beg your pardon...I didn't quite catch that," said Mrs. Atwell cupping her ear in her hand.

"No mother," he groaned.

She blinked at him in mock surprise, "I'm sorry...who?"

Dominic groaned and rolled his eyes, "Mrs. Atwell," he said reluctantly.

"That's better...now where were we?" she asked and turned back to the board. "If you could take out your books," she said as she flipped the sheet of paper over the top of the easel to reveal a blank page.

Dominic opened the small bag which sat by his chair, and he pulled an exercise book and pencil case from inside. He placed the objects before him on the table while his mother wrote on the board. Her words echoed around the kitchen and Dominic realised with a spreading horror that she was talking...no not just talking, but teaching. He absently tore a small piece of paper from the book and popped it into his mouth as he watched her hands move across the easel. Numbers and figures bounced over the sheet of paper as he chewed while his fingers absently pulled at the end of a clear pen. Mrs. Atwell continued to speak, her attention focused on the paper as she wrote quickly on the sheet, her words reaching into the kitchen to unhearing ears. Dominic watched his mother as she moved at lightning speed across the paper and allowed his hands to moved unconsciously toward his mouth where he placed the now empty pen barrel between his lips and expertly positioned the ball of wet paper into the cartridge and...

The ball of spit spun in the air as it flew from the empty pen and through the expanse of the kitchen. Dominic hadn't even realised what he was doing until after it had happened and he watched in horror as the ball of spit flew through the air toward the figure of his mother...

Chapter 4
BULL(E) DOZER

Mr. Atwell walked through the front door and hung his jacket at the end of the bannister. His mood was jovial as he surveyed his surroundings and with a smile on his face he stalked his way along the hall to the kitchen before flinging open the door to the kitchen and almost bounding through the threshold into the white interior beyond. "How're my favourite two people in all the world!" he exclaimed as he flung his open arms in anticipation of the embracing hug of his beloved wife and son....

Instead, he was greeted by his wife sitting in silence at the table, her face a mixture of anger and remorse. He looked around the kitchen in confusion at the expanding scene unfolding before his eyes. Books lay discarded on the kitchen table, an abandoned chair lay overturned and sprawled across the floor...the easel stood with unwritten words on the table, a position it had assumed since the morning ...in the center of the hard-wooden surface sat a small crumpled ball of paper. Mr. Atwell looked about the room for a moment and raised his finger, "Dominic?" The question hung in the air for a moment, and Mr. Atwell watched as the colour in his wife's cheeks turned a crimson red as anger coursed through her veins.

"That...that monster!" she fumed.

"Dominic..."

"Yes!" snapped Mrs. Atwell. "Who else would I be talking about!" she fumed. "Do you know what he did?" the anger and tone were growing as she was talking and Mr. Atwell took a slight step backward and felt his back press against the wall. "He...and I...I was there...and he..." her hands were a flurry of movement, waving through the air as she struggled to find the words to express her anger. "The math...writing...I was writing...yes, I was writing and he...he...he..." her hands followed her words and Mr. Atwell watched as she mimed her actions. "Across the room... his own mother...back of the neck...his mother...me...his mother...his own mother!" her words were rising to a crescendo as she continued her tale.

"Woah! Woah! Woah!" urged Mr. Atwell as he stepped forward toward his wife, his hands held before him as a guard. "Take it easy love," he smiled as he spoke.

"Take it easy!" she snapped, repeating her husband's mantra. "Take it easy! Do you know..." she slowed and took a deep breath as anger flashed over her face. "That monster" she glanced up at the ceiling as the words fell from her mouth. "I was writing...and he...he..." she could feel the anger rising again as she attempted to tell her story. "A ball of spit...right on the back of my neck... his own mother!" she trailed off into a wail.

"Let me get this straight," spoke Mr. Atwell slowly and carefully, stifling a grin behind his frown. "You were teaching Dominic...our son, and while your back was turned he shot you with a spitball?" She nodded as he stood watching her, then as a smile broke across Mr. Atwell's face.

"It's not funny!" she stormed.

"Yes, it is."

"No...it's not even remotely funny."

"Not even just a little bit?" said Mr. Atwell, raising his hand and offering his index finger and thumb in a pinching movement.

"Not even a smidgeon!" Despite his best intentions, Mr. Atwell could not fight the laughter spilling up his throat as she flushed a deep crimson. "Well, laugh this up clown, tomorrow that little horror upstairs will be going to work with you." The smile faded on his face as she spoke, "Not so funny now, are we?" she smirked at his discomfort.

"Oh no!" protested Mr. Atwell, shaking his hands before him. "You know as well as anyone…a building site is no place for a child."

"Child! He's a monster!" fumed Mrs. Atwell.

Dominic sat in the dark of his bedroom and listened through the silence as the sounds of his parents arguing wafted up the stairs to his bedroom. He listened for a moment before he finally collapsed on the bed and rolled onto his back gazing at the ceiling. The different tones of white swirled and mixed into one large tsunami of white as it spread its wings across the expanse of the ceiling. He struggled to remember the events which had led to his sudden expulsion to his room. He remembered the ball hitting his mother, but he couldn't remember placing the paper in his mouth. He could remember the anger of his mother…then the tears… her tears, the hurt in her eyes as she watched him while he sat and innocently blamed someone else…"it wasn't me…" had he even said that? He was the only one in the room, who else could it have been? Everything else had been a blur…his mother shouting…him knocking over the chair and kicking out at the door… her words echoing in his ears as he ran up to his room….

Dominic turned onto his side and stared at the posters on the wall as they blurred through his welling tears. He couldn't understand why he did what he did, he couldn't understand what made him do the things he did. He buried his head into his pillow as he struggled to contain his tears and succumbed to a loud sob which erupted through his body. He forced himself to stop as he heard footsteps on the stairs outside his door. "Dom?" the voice of his father reached through the wooden barrier and was accompanied by three slight knocks. He sat up in bed and looked at the door as it was pushed open slightly and as light spilled in through the open crack of the door, the round face of Mr. Atwell forced its way through into the room. "You okay?" he asked and watched as his son forced a small nod in his direction. Mr. Atwell took this as a sign to enter the room, and he placed himself at the foot of the bed, taking a seat on the corner of the bed. The duvet pushed up around his body as his father sank into the warm comfort of the blankets and he looked at Dominic, smiling through a frowned expression. "Good news, son," he said slowly. "Tomorrow how do you fancy coming to work with me?" Dominic knew the words were more of a statement than a question and the fact of the matter was he wouldn't have much of a choice. Reluctantly, Dominic nodded and watched his dad as a smile broke across his face.

"You up lad?" shouted Mr. Atwell from outside Dominic's door. Dominic forced his eyes open, and he gazed at the clock which was sitting on the edge of his dressing table.

"Seven," he moaned to himself as he pulled himself into a sitting position in his bed.

The harsh sound of knocking erupted further on the door outside his room. "Time to get up, we'll be leaving in forty minutes," said his father's voice. Dominic sighed and pulled himself out of bed and stared at the back of the door for a moment before forcing himself across the floor. The weight of his legs felt heavy with every step he took toward the bedroom door, and slowly he forced himself out of the room and allowed the cold air of the hall to strike him as he shuffled in quiet dread to the day ahead.

The journey was cold and long as Dominic sat at the front of his father's white van. Occasionally he would glance over at his father who was intent on staring ahead, whistling in tune to the sounds drifting through the cab from the radio. He shifted in his seat and pushed several pieces of paper from the old leather bound seat onto the floor of the vehicle and stared balefully out of the window, unsure what to expect at his father's work. He remembered the conversation between his parents the previous night and thought about his dad's words. "A building site is no place for a young boy...." he had said. Dominic had to admit to himself that a slight sense of thrill was coursing through his veins at the thought of going to work with his father, not just for the large tools and the heavy equipment, but for a chance to see what his father did for a career. The van turned the corner, and Dominic was brought from his daydream by the sharp, shrill noise of the van's horn as his father hit the center of the steering wheel and waved at a group of men walking across the muddy ground. The van slowed to a stop outside a small plain portacabin, and Dominic sat for a moment before he realised that his father had turned the van off and jumped out of the van. "Come on boy!" he called back over his shoulder as he walked toward the building without looking back.

Dominic struggled for a moment with his seatbelt, then jumped from the cab into the mud around his feet. He looked about the building site...at the men...the vehicles...the equipment and materials. Men were already at work, shoveling and hammering and moving material from one part of the yard to another where other men pulled and cut and lifted and nailed a variety of wood, brick, and metal into place. "Get in here!" the sound of his father's voice cut through the noise of the building site. Jumping at the tone of his voice, Dominic sprinted across the yard, mud and water splashing up against his boots as he ran until he reached the door of the hut. He could feel as his father's eyes bore into his body as he stood framed in the doorway. Gingerly he stepped into the hut under the scrutiny of his father and two workmates.

"Tommo…Steve," he said pointing toward Dominic as he walked across the office. "This is my son," he said beaming at the men. "He's spending the day with us today."

"Why ain't he at school?" queried the smaller of the men.

"Don't you worry about that," replied his father. "This is like work experience." The two men nodded with the explanation, and the three of them turned to the desk where Dominic's father began to pour over a set of blueprints. Pointing to several points across the paper, he began to whisper sets of instructions to the other two men, who in turn nodded and cast their own gaze over the paper spread before them. Dominic sat on a small chair in the corner of the office and sighed…bored. He looked around the walls at various pictures and charts stuck across the walls. Calendars mixed with graphs and figures of declining and rising profit margins, as various pieces of furniture sat against the walls from soft furnishings to a sturdy metal filing cabinet with an adorning plant sat on top, spreading its foliage and spilling over the edges of the plant pot. Dominic stood and walked toward the filing cabinet where his eyes were drawn to a small plaque hanging on the wall close to it. Slowly and carefully he read the labels which stretched across the wooden surface of the plaque. Small sets of keys hung from each of the hooks fastened to the plaque, and Dominic mouthed the inscriptions on the labels which accompanied each key, from tool shed to bulldozer to toilet block to main gates. A burst of laughter disturbed his thoughts, and he sighed again and looked over at his father who was shaking hands with the men before slapping them on the shoulder and taking his place behind the desk. The men collected their hard helmets and walked out of the office into the cold morning air.

The morning had gone slowly for Dominic who sat gazing out of the window for much of it as he watched the men outside scurry past as they worked. His father had largely ignored his presence and occasionally would look up from his desk and nod toward the boy. He glanced at the clock on the desk and sighed again as the small numbers ticked slowly toward twelve. He returned to his lonely and quiet vigil of the world outside and sighed heavily with boredom. "It's no good," remarked his father, eventually rising from his chair. "I've gotta go, and when you gotta go, you gotta go," He laughed as he walked across the hut. He glanced around the office for a moment before turning to Dominic. "You see my paper?" he asked as he grabbed his hard hat. Dominic briefly glanced about the office before shaking his head. "Oh well," groaned his father reluctantly, his hand resting on the handle of his office. Pushing the door open he called out into the cold air, "Anybody got a paper?" Without waiting for an answer, he stepped out into the muddy worksite. Dominic watched for a moment as his father walked across the site, pausing briefly at a pile of boxes before changing direction for a small blue portable toilet in the corner of the site. With his father out of sight, he leapt from his chair and grabbed his jacket which lay limply on a plush chair by the filing cabinet. He pulled the coat over his body, pulling the zip up under his chin. He had decided he had had enough of this boredom…it was time he left and went home.

His eyes strayed to the plaque on the wall for a moment and locked onto a set of keys…a single set. The label read Bulldozer…

Chapter Five

NEW NEWS

Mr. Atwell walked across the muddy ground of the building site grumbling under his breath about his missing newspaper and his son sitting alone in the office. "Has anyone got a paper?" he called out into the air as he walked, while his eyes flicked about the yard. His eyes wandered to a small pile of boxes which sat on the ground amongst piles of bricks and wood. A folded paper sat on top of an open box, its pages folded and scrunched as it lay over the contents of the crate. "That'll do," said Mr. Atwell to himself as he picked his way through the mud. His hand touched the paper and his fingers curled around the newspaper, before he thrust it firmly beneath his arm, then adjusting his protective hard helmet he splashed across the site toward the lonely standing cubicle at the edge of the yard. He grasped at the handle and pushed open the door, glancing back over his shoulder and shouting to no-one and everyone, "Don't disturb me for the next ten minutes!" Then he disappeared into the toilet.

The seat of the toilet was cold and hard, and Mr. Atwell shuffled uncomfortably on the plastic rim as he settled into position. The confines of the cubicle were cramped, and the smell which emanated from the chemical toilet was unpleasant, causing Mr. Atwell to wrinkle his nose in disgust. He rested his arms on his knees and unfolded the newspaper and spread it out before him. "Simian Times," he murmured at the banner cast in red at the top of the front page. "Never heard of it," he grumbled as his eyes flicked over the headline which stood out in big bold black letters across the white paper.

"Banana shortage," declared the banner and Mr. Atwell frowned at the headline, shrugged and continued to read, murmuring to himself as the words leapt out of the page at him. "Banana shortage, must be a slow news day," he chuckled at his own comment and continued to read the main story. "World council officials are concerned about a shortage of bananas over the coming months, sources declare," he whispered as he sat on the porcelain throne. "Better pop to the shops on the way home," he mused as he opened the pages of the newspaper, his eyes flicking over the stories inside. His fingers ruffled the pages as he swept through the paper headlines. "World crisis threatens Borneo rainforest...Who flung the dung?...The fastest primate on the planet...Conservation or preservation." "What kind of paper is this?" complained Mr. Atwell as he flicked through the pages. As he continued to read he became aware of a noise outside...a roar of an engine, but in his present position he swept the thought to the back of his mind....

Dominic pulled his body up onto the frame of the heavy red bulldozer which sat patiently in the building site. His fingers curled around the small silver set of keys which rested in his fist. He could feel their cold touch cut into the palm of his hand and he sighed as they spoke to him, silently through his mind urging him to start the engine and drive the behemoth through the site. He shivered as the cold bit into his body and his hand shook as he fumbled with the key against the ignition before gently sliding the metal into the barrel. Turning the key, he listened in silent bliss as the engine roared into life. He could see the noise of the engine had attracted the stares from some of the men on the site, while others were waving and shouting toward the vehicle. The words and the meanings were lost on the boy as the engine purred and throbbed beneath his body and Dominic placed his hand on the large gearstick which rose toward him from the floor of the vehicle. He could see men running toward the bulldozer, and a grin spread across his face as a cheer erupted involuntarily from his throat as his fist pumped enthusiastically in the air.

The heavy machinery slowly lurched under the weight of its own momentum and juddered across the muddy surface of the ground. The tracks beneath the cab churned at the mud and toiled massive grooves into the soft surface as it crawled its way over the building site....

Mr. Atwell was lost in thought as his eyes caught sight of a small advertisement in the corner of the paper, surrounded by stories of the loudest howl in Africa and a special profile of apes in space. His mind was aware of a commotion outside, and he could vaguely hear shouting and the thunderous roar of an engine but was instead fixed on the words which now were filtering into his mind from the small boxed advert.

"Do you have an exceptional child?" the advert asked, to which Mr. Atwell subconsciously nodded. "...misunderstood... special?" again Mr. Atwell found himself nodding, whilst outside the commotion was growing stronger and louder. "Then here at Hazeldene, we embrace your child's nature and nurture it, helping them to find their inner and true self. If you have nowhere left to turn and have a special child...then call us here at Hazeldene now!"

"Hazeldene," murmured Mr. Atwell quietly to himself, before he suddenly became aware of the noise outside the portable toilet. He stood, pulling his trousers part way up his legs and opened the door, "What is going on?!" His words trailed off as he watched helplessly as the lumbering form of the bulldozer bore down upon the toilet. He quickly slammed the door shut and placed his hands on the back of the door. Taking his place once again sitting on the toilet, he closed his eyes, bracing for impact.

The Bulldozer hit the side of the toilet sending it crashing to the floor, Dominic's father spilling from the cubicle, his trousers wrapped around his feet and covered in a mass of dirty brown liquid. "Dominic!" he roared, his face turning a deep crimson as he lay on the ground covered with the excrement and water from the toilet.

Chapter Six

MISS HAWTHORNE

Miss Hawthorne sat at her large oak table and gazed over the vast array of paper which lay sprawled across the heavy wooden surface. Financial figures and charts stared back at her in stubborn defiance to her glare. "I really don't know where to start or what to do," she admitted, spinning her chair from the table and for a moment looking over the grounds. She sighed heavily and rested her head into her hands. She could feel a wave of desperation sweep over her and swell up inside her as she spun back around to face the piling bills and accounts on the desk. She lifted one after another, casting her gaze across the myriad of numbers which streamed over the paper. Piece after piece, number after number, she felt as though she were drowning in figures. She took off her glasses and placed them carefully on the desk amidst a pile of paper. She stood from her chair, resting her hands on the edge of the table before moving slowly across the floor until she finally came to a halt before an ornate fireplace with a large portrait of an elderly man above the finely sculpted marble.

"Father…what am I to do?" she asked the painting softly. His eyes stared down at her as she gazed up at him as though expecting an answer. "This house…this school…it's not just my home, it's my life," she moaned. "Everything I have ever known is in this house," her hand ran along the top of the fireplace as she spoke, while her eyes never left her father's, as he gazed from his portrait. "I can remember Christmases in this room as a child," she spoke wistfully as her eyes glazed over. "The beauty…the decorations. Mother decorating the tree while you sat in your chair by the fire laughing at us as we struggled with the tinsel," her smile faded with the memories. "The good times…the birthdays, the laughter. Oh, father the house was a home back then. Why did it all have to change?" she bemoaned. "Why do we have to grow up? Back then it was so simple," she said as her eyes fell to the floor and watched as the slight splash of water fell from her eyes and onto the hearth at her feet. "Things seemed so easy when I was a child."

"They always do, honey," came a soft voice from the doorway.

"Eronymous!" said Miss Hawthorne, jumping slightly at the sound of his voice. "I didn't hear you come in."

"I am sorry my dear," he apologized. "But you seemed so…" he struggled to find the right words to ease her pain.

"It's alright," she said softly, wiping away her tears, "I was just thinking out loud."

"I heard," admitted Eronymous Hindle and shifted his eyes downward, embarrassed by his interference in her remorse. "It will be alright…" began Hindle.

"How do you know!" snapped Miss Hawthorne. "How can you be so sure? You…you can't just wave a magic wand and make all of this disappear." She walked to the desk as she spoke and as her words struck Mr. Hindle, the sheaves of paper were flung in the air from the surface of the table. She collapsed in her chair and buried her head in her hands, shying away from her friend's gaze.

"Olivia," he said softly.

"Leave me," she stated.

"Olivia."

"Please leave me."

"I'm sorry my dear, but I've no intention of going anywhere," he moved further into the room and walked carefully over to the desk, picking his way through the cavalcade of paper which now lay sprawled across the floor. He looked down at her gently and smiled. "We are in this together," he said softly and smiled as she raised her head to face him. "I won't let you go through this alone, and we will find a way," he promised.

Miss Hawthorne shook her head. "No, we won't Eronymous. This is it," she said sadly. "After this year we will both have to find somewhere else to live."

"No...no...no...that's just it my dear," urged Hindle, a grin spreading across his face. "We won't have to."

"Yes we will," said Miss Hawthorne. "The bank..."

"This is what I am trying to tell you..." he stood before her, his voice rising as he became excited. "We've had a phone call."

"Eronymous...Eronymous...please slow down...I don't understand, you're not making any sense."

"That's just it Olivia, we've had a phone call. We'll be alright."

"Please calm yourself and explain," she said firmly.

"Yes...yes..." he enthused. "You see, all this...the phone call" he was becoming excited again as he spoke.

"Mr. Hindle, please!" snapped Miss Hawthorne. "From the beginning."

"What...oh...yes...sorry," he apologized, taking a seat and breathing deeply to regain his composure. "We've had a phone call from a Mr. Atwell...he wants to send his son here...to Hazeldene," he allowed his words to sink in for a moment before gazing at Miss Hawthorne wildly. "They are coming to visit tomorrow morning with a view to enrolling their son in our school, my dear," he smiled at her and leant across the desk. Taking her hands in his own, he whispered, "Hazeldene is saved."

Chapter Seven
MONEY FOR NOTHING

Mr. Atwell sat in the office and shuffled uncomfortably in his chair. His hand snaked to his throat where he could feel the constriction around his neck caused by the tightly donned red tie which hung limply down the front of his white shirt. He pulled at the item of clothing and moved his head as he felt strangled by the object. A subtle glance from his wife stopped his fidgeting, and he subconsciously raised his hand to his nose as he sniffed his fingers. He could still smell the odour of the refuse from the toilet on his skin as he ran his fingers beneath his nose, despite several showers and the entire contents of a full bottle of shower gel. He cast an angry glance toward his son, who much like himself was sitting fidgeting in his chair by the large ornate desk, while dressed in a smart suit. He placed his hand on his knees with another sharp glance from Mrs. Atwell, and while he waited his thoughts drifted back to the previous day...the newspaper...the toilet and the... the...the...he flushed with anger as he remembered being covered in sewage, and any thoughts of guilt about sending his son to this school soon disappeared.

He remembered the drive home, with paper strewn across the seat of the van and his son leaning out of the window gasping for air against the rising stink in the cab. He remembered as the cold bit into his body as he shivered under the weight of the dirty brown moisture which covered him. He shivered as he thought of the stodgy brown objects which covered his body under the weight of the water in the toilet system as he climbed out of the wreckage of the cubicle. He recalled standing amidst the laughter from his employees, while the bulldozer continued its journey through the worksite until it came to a rest, buried beneath a pile of rubble from a recently built wall. He remembered standing in the passage of his home, while his wife laid papers at his feet while he peeled the wet clothing from his body, watching as they fell onto the wooden flooring, then slamming up the stairs; naked and angry. As the water from the shower flowed over his body, he decided Hazeldene was the answer…whatever the cost. It had taken little in the way of argument to persuade his wife about the prospect of sending Dominic away to the school, and by that evening they had arranged an appointment with the proprietors of Hazeldene.

He pulled a small piece of paper from his pocket and glanced down at the words written hastily across the lines: Miss Olivia Hawthorne, headmistress, and owner; Mr. Eronymous Hindle, deputy headmaster. He briefly wondered how they would receive and cope with their son. He had spent the night searching the internet for reviews about the school, but had found very little…even the paper he had found at the building site had no website, so they still had very little knowledge about the school.

They had arrived early that day to be answered at the door of the school by a small man, with a large round body. He had frowned upon their arrival, but had seemed pleasant enough and shown them through the hallway to the main office and asked them to wait with a smile and brief nod before he had rushed out of the room. Now here they sat, waiting for a formal interview with Miss Hawthorne.

Eronymous shuffled from foot to foot outside the door, and Miss Hawthorne strode confidently along the hallway toward the office. "Mr. Hindle," she smiled as she spoke and held her hands out toward him as she approached. "Are they here?" She craned her neck toward the closed door as she took his hands in her own.

"Well...yes," stumbled Mr. Hindle, glancing back toward the closed door. She could see small pearls of sweat forming on his brow as he spoke.

"What is it?" she asked staring into his eyes.

"Now Olivia...before we start, can I just point out that this is not my fault...I mean, how could I have known?" he stammered.

"Come now, Eronymous. What on earth are you talking about?" she laughed slightly at his words.

"Well...you see...on the phone..." he staggered through his words before taking a deep breath. "Before we go in you must promise not to overreact."

"You're being silly now," she chided him playfully and pulled her hands from his, reaching for the handle of the door.

"Please Olivia...these people..."

"Come now," she was beginning to lose patience with his attitude and pushed her way past. "We deal with all sorts, you know that. There is nothing behind this door that I have not dealt with before." Her hand closed on the doorknob, and she turned the handle and threw open the door to the office and stared at the couple sitting with their son before her desk. She stood for a moment, frozen on the spot before regaining her composure and stepping across the threshold of the office toward the desk. She took a quick glance toward Mr. Hindle as she moved silently across the carpeted floor and took her seat at the desk opposite the family. She smiled and adjusted her glasses slightly before speaking, "You are..." she hazarded slowly, her eyes reaching down to a small pad of paper sitting on her desk.

"Atwell," the father spoke and smiled at her, reaching out a hand across the desk in her direction. Miss Hawthorne smiled back at him and shook it warmly, before accepting his wife's hand. "And this is Dominic," the father presented his son, nodding in Dominic's direction as he sat by his mother.

"It is a pleasure to meet you all," said Miss Hawthorne, glancing from the family to Mr. Hindle and back again. "But, there seems to be a problem here," she commented, looking toward Mr. Hindle again. Promptly rising from her chair, she ushered her deputy out of the office and into the hall.

Mr. Atwell sat dumbstruck for a moment and looked at his wife. "Well, that didn't go well," he eventually admitted, frowning and replaying everything in his head as though attempting to find something they had done wrong to offend the woman. Indeed, when the door had first opened, he had been struck with a sublime beauty from the slim woman as she crossed the floor. Her clothes had clung to her body as she moved and he swallowed guiltily and glanced at his wife and smiled at her. What if the woman had sensed his eyes crossing her body? Was it his fault? He looked at his son…no…definitely the boy's fault, he concluded. No matter where they took Dominic, the boy would get into trouble just by being Dominic. "What have you done, boy?" he demanded, looking at the bewildered child.

"Who are these…these…these…people?" demanded Miss Hawthorne in an urgent whisper, her hands rubbing the sides of her head.

"I did try to warn you," apologized Mr. Hindle, as they stood outside the office whispering.

"Look at them!" she whispered, bending and peering through the lock of the office. "Just look…they're…they're…" she struggled to find the words and straightened, kicking out at a potted plant by the door.

"Normal," concluded Mr. Hindle calmly. He continued, "Please Olivia, I was not to know. We received the phone call yesterday afternoon about a potential new student. I had no way of knowing…I mean our usual clientele contact us through the same means."

Miss Hawthorne sighed, turned, looked at him, placed a hand on his arm and smiled. "I know, it's not your fault," she admitted, before turning back to the closed door as though she could peer through the wooden obstacle.

"My only thought was for you and Hazeldene, and its future," he rubbed his hands together as he spoke. "I'm sorry," he said eventually.

"No, Eronymous," she said softly. "You did what you thought was right," she sighed and gripped the handle. "We will just have to tell them that this is a mistake and send them on their way." She pushed open the door and strode purposely across the floor of the office and stared at the family from her seat while Mr. Hindle stood by the door.

The room was filled with silence for a few minutes as Miss Hawthorne toyed with the papers at her fingertips before she spoke again. "Mr. and Mrs. Atwell, I'm afraid there has been an error of judgement on our behalf," she began. "Your son…"

"Please, Miss Hawthorne," interrupted Mr. Atwell firmly. "Your advertisement said you accept 'gifted' children and our son is special," he leant forward as he spoke. "Every school he has attended has failed to cope with his special needs, and like your advert said, you embrace uniqueness."

"Yes, quite, and where, may I ask did you see our advertisement?" said Miss Hawthorne uncomfortably.

"I dunno," admitted Mr. Atwell. "I found this paper on my

building site," as he spoke he caught Miss Hawthorne glance toward Mr. Hindle at the door, frowning at her deputy.

"You see Mr. Atwell, we cater to a specific clientele, and I feel your son…would not fit in." She looked Dominic up and down as she spoke.

"Excuse me!" snapped Mrs. Atwell, slamming her hands on the arm of her chair. "My Dominic is just as good as any other boy or girl you have in this school."

"No, it's not that…" stammered Miss Hawthorne, but Mrs. Atwell had no intention of stopping.

"He may not have a silver spoon shoved in his mouth, but he is as bright and smart as anyone else here!"

"Please Mrs. Atwell," stated Miss Hawthorne firmly. "It was not my intention to cause any offence, I simply do not think Dominic here would settle in with the other children. You see here at Hazeldene, we cater to an elite and unique custom who expect a certain level of discretion and education. Looking at Dominic, I don't think he would be very happy under our tutelage."

"We shall be the ones who decide that Miss Hawthorne!" snapped Mrs. Atwell.

"Please," said Mr. Atwell, calmly placing a hand on his wife's arm and smiling at her. "I think I know what Miss Hawthorne here is alluding to…." he smiled at Mrs. Atwell, then turned his smile to face Miss Hawthorne. "Don't worry, Miss Hawthorne," he spoke gently as he reached into his jacket pocket. "We have money."

"Mr. Atwell, this is not about money."

"Status?" he asked, raising his eyebrows in mock surprise. "If that's what you're worried about, let me assure you, I own my own business which, might I add, is doing very well for itself. We may not be your usual high society personage, but we do have money" he assured her and placed a chequebook before her on the desk. "Name your price…."

"Please Mr. Atwell, it's not the money or the status, I simply don't think your son would like it here," stammered Miss Hawthorne, desperately looking between the two parents.

"I will not take no for an answer, Miss Hawthorne," said Mr. Atwell firmly. "Now…name your price," he said again.

Mr. Hindle hurried across the floor and leant close to her ear and whispered, "It is unorthodox my dear, but think of the future of Hazeldene."

Miss Hawthorne paused and looked between the adults for a moment. The seconds seemed to pass slowly as her eyes drifted over each one in turn, from Mr. Hindle nodding at her to Mr. and Mrs. Atwell who were watching her nervously while waiting for an answer. Eventually, she stood and smiled at Mr. Atwell and extended a hand in his direction. "Congratulations," she said smiling and shook his hand firmly, then looked at Dominic and smiled in his direction. "Welcome to Hazeldene!"

Chapter Eight
SKOOL RULEZ

Dominic watched as his parents signed the cheque and shook the woman's hand. "Pleasure doing business with you," oozed Mr. Atwell as the ink-stained the pages of his open chequebook. "Dominic can start straight away," his words were almost dismissive as he concentrated on his writing.

"Don't worry," reassured Miss Hawthorne as she watched Mr. Atwell write. "You can bring him back in a couple of days with his belongings."

"That's alright," said Mrs. Atwell standing from her chair. "We have his case in the car."

"Oh," commented Miss Hawthorne, taken slightly aback by the statement. "Very well," she said and turned to Mr. Hindle. "Can you inform the staff that we have a new pupil?" she continued cautiously. "And inform the teachers of his special needs."

Dominic watched her talking to Mr. Hindle as he remained sitting in his chair and smirked to himself, inwardly shrugging. Another school…another set of teachers…he thought to himself while he watched as his father rose to his feet and moved toward the door, announcing that he would retrieve the case from the car. He sighed and decided in his own mind…two weeks…that's how long it would be before he was home…two weeks. There wasn't a school that could hold me, he thought brashly and sat smirking at the adults while swinging his legs in the chair. His father had returned from the car with a large battered brown case and placed it unceremoniously by the desk. "One case!" he declared happily and turned to look down at his son. He smiled briefly at him and ran his fingers through the boy's hair. "Well, lad," he said. "This is it…good luck." He turned away from his son and walked briskly for the door, "We'll be back at the end of summer term," he called over his shoulder, then looked back at Miss Hawthorne. "And please, if you need more money because of the boy…do not hesitate to call," he said smoothly. With that, he walked from the office and out toward the open front door.

"Dominic," came the soft voice of his mother. He turned to look at her and could see the regret in her eyes as she spoke. "My little man," she smiled as she looked at him and Dominic watched as a single tear fell from her eye and draped itself across her cheek.

"Mother," he said quietly.

"Be brave," Mrs. Atwell said as the tears filled up her eyes. "Mummy will always be here for you," she promised. "Just call…" she straightened and wiped her eyes and followed her husband from the room, closing the door behind her without looking back.

"Dominic," began Miss Hawthorne looking at the boy sitting alone in her office. "Are you alright?" she asked. Dominic nodded and watched her every movement as she placed herself in the large chair behind her desk. He didn't know whether he liked this woman yet, he reflected as he stared at her. "Now," she began looking at several pieces of paper on her desk. "Neither of us was expecting you to start immediately," she offered, looking earnestly at him. "I have so much to prepare…so many teachers, so many lessons to prepare for you," her eyes locked on his as she spoke. "You must be prepared as much as I."

"I don't care," said Dominic defiantly. "One school's as much as the next."

"But you will," said Miss Hawthorne kindly, then suddenly changed her whole demeanor. Her voice hardened as she spoke, "We have rules."

"I know...I know," complained Dominic sighing. "No running...no swearing..."

"Please, Mr. Atwell," interjected Miss Hawthorne, holding up her hand. "If you could show some decorum in your attitude."

"I'm sorry," he mumbled. "It's just I've been to a lot of schools, and I've heard the same thing over and over...don't do this, don't do that, you kind of get used to that sort of thing."

"Yes, well here at Hazeldene we do things a little bit differently," replied Miss Hawthorne curtly, as she perched herself on the edge of the table. "We do have rules here...and we do expect you to follow these rules at all times, but they are probably not what you would find at other schools. What we run here at Hazeldene is a unique learning experience for children with special needs and abilities, and we find that certain pupils require additional help," she smiled as she looked at him. "While we do not advocate running in the halls, it may be necessary for some species. We do not permit either climbing or defecation in the hallways," she said sternly. "No sitting on desks, the chairs are there for a reason. All pupils must adhere to the correct dress code..." her words droned on, and Dominic frowned. What the hell was she talking about? No climbing...no pooing...sit on chairs, was this woman for real, he thought, or was this a dream? He shook his head and realised she was still talking. "You are not listening, are you, Mr. Atwell? Not a good start, but don't worry, all of our rules are clearly presented throughout the school."

"I'm sorry," apologized Dominic politely. He shrugged inwardly to himself... rules...he wouldn't be here long enough to worry about the rules, and he smiled sweetly at her.

"Very good," cooed Miss Hawthorne as she looked at the door as it opened slightly. "Ah! Mr. Hindle," she announced.

"The teachers have been…warned about our new pupil," he looked at Dominic and smiled.

"Excellent!" clapped Miss Hawthorne. "Then I think Mr. Atwell, we should go and meet your first teacher!" She leapt down from the edge of the desk and crossed to the door and held it wide open for Dominic to follow her out into the school. "Let's meet your teacher!" she laughed and looked at him as he walked across the office. "I hope for your sake, Mr. Atwell, that you enjoy your stay here at Hazeldene."

Dominic walked slowly along the hallway behind Mr. Hindle and Miss Hawthorne as they walked before him and he attempted to see in each room as they walked. The windows were set high in the door and all Dominic could make out was the ceiling in each of the classrooms that they passed.

"Which class have you placed Dominic with?" asked Miss Hawthorne, glancing at the sheet which Mr. Hindle had just passed to her.

"I have placed him in the Borneo house," replied Mr. Hindle. "They are about the same age group as Dominic here, and I think the similarities between our new pupil and the majority of the class will be beneficial."

"Ah yes," concluded Miss Hawthorne looking at the paper in her hands. "Many of the pupils in the group are of the…same genii." She briefly glanced back at Dominic as she spoke. Her attention was soon drawn back to the paper. "Which class is currently running?" she asked.

"Social studies," replied Mr. Hindle curtly.

"Perfect…something easy for you to participate in," Miss

Hawthorne called over her shoulder. "And you should like Miss Gibson. She's a lovely lady," she laughed and looked at Mr. Hindle as she spoke, who in turn laughed at her comment. Dominic didn't like the sound of that. Usually, it meant the teacher was either tough or a bully, and he gulped as they stopped suddenly outside a door. "Here we are," commented Miss Hawthorne and knocked briskly on the door.

"Come!" the voice from the other side of the door was high pitched as it drifted through into the hall. Miss Hawthorne grasped at the handle and turned the silver knob in her hand, then pushed the door open. "Remember children," came the high-pitched voice, "this is a new pupil to our school, and while he may look different, we expect you all to treat him with respect."

"Yes, Miss Gibson," came the chorused reply from the children. Mr. Hindle waved Dominic to a stop outside the room as Miss Hawthorne strode into the class.

"Miss Gibson…children," said Miss Hawthorne politely. Dominic could hear her words from outside the room as the words fell through the partially open door.

"Good morning Miss Hawthorne," again the chorus of voices rang through the hall.

"Now, children, remember that we operate a strict rule here at Hazeldene of absolute respect to everyone…no matter what species," spoke Miss Hawthorne.

"Yes Miss Hawthorne," came the chorus.

"And I would expect the same level of respect to be shown to our new pupil…" she paused briefly. "I must warn you, he is a little different from the usual student that we accept, but nevertheless we are all here to learn, and I would expect the same common courtesy that you would extend to your fellow students. Do you understand?"

"Yes, Miss Hawthorne."

"Then...Mr. Hindle," called Miss Hawthorne.

The door was pushed open, and Dominic was pushed into the room by Mr. Hindle who whispered in his ear as he pushed him into the class, "Good luck, son."

Dominic stood in the doorway and stared around the room at his classmates and teacher with a sense of shock growing over his body. This couldn't be...surely...he was dreaming...

"Dominic..." said Miss Hawthorne softly. "These are your new classmates."

Dominic stared around at the children and met each gaze in turn with astonishment. These weren't children...they were apes. Then everything went black....

Chapter Nine

MONKEYING AROUND

Everything was in a haze as Dominic opened his eyes slowly and examined the room in which he was laying. The bed he was on was hard and cold, and his hands could feel a clammy plastic covering beneath his body. He felt cold and confused as he tried to sit up on the bed and look at the blurred figures speaking at the end of the room. From his position, he could hear the distant voices talking about him and their concerns over his mental condition, and he tried to move to see who the people were. Had Miss Hawthorne called his parents back, he wondered briefly but struggled to hear their voices. He could hear Miss Hawthorne talking to a woman who he did not recognise, and he groaned as he attempted to sit up in bed, before slumping back to the cold plastic covering of the bed. "He's awake," said the female voice that he did not recognise and his thoughts drifted back to the classroom as he struggled to remember what had happened.

He remembered the door opening and walking in through the door-frame behind Miss Hawthorne and seeing a gibbon standing at the front of the class with a small set of half-moon glasses perched on the end of its stubby black nose. He could imagine the bright shiny black eyes staring at him from her white lined furred ringed face. Her long arm was frozen in his memory stretching up onto a blackboard with a single piece of chalk while her other arm held in place a small red textbook. He frowned as he remembered the clothes she was wearing...a white blouse with a high ruffled collar beneath a light coloured cardigan and a straight blue pencil skirt. His thoughts strayed to the class of children who sat staring at him as he stood behind Miss Hawthorne. He could see their faces...chimps, gorillas, tamarins, lemurs, mandrills and some others he hadn't recognised...then his head swam and...here he was.

"Now, now Dominic," came the soothing voice of Miss Hawthorne as she peered over his prone body.

"Take it easy son, you've had quite a fright and given us all a bit of a turn," the second voice was that of Mr. Hindle as he leaned forward to look at the boy.

"Please...do not crowd my patient," snapped a harsh voice from the rear of the room. Dominic strained to see the third person but struggled to see past the headmistress and her deputy. He could see the shadow of a large figure at the rear, but as the voice continued he realised it had come from elsewhere in the room. "He's had quite a shock and will need time to recover his wits," she said as Dominic still searched for her. "And I think a proper explanation is called for." This was aimed at Miss Hawthorne who blushed slightly at the inference.

"Yes...quite," said the headmistress slowly who turned to smile at Dominic. "I am sorry Dominic," she apologized. "I haven't been completely honest with you," she admitted glancing at Mr. Hindle for support. "You see, here at Hazeldene, we cater to a different class of pupil than you are usually associated with. A unique learning experience set in the rural confines of Britain and away from the prying eyes of the world. A place where your child can develop and explore his or her own personality, whilst experiencing some of the best teachers the Simian world can offer." Her words came straight from a prospectus, thought Dominic, as he listened to her speech. "In short Mr. Atwell…we are a school for apes and monkeys," she paused as her words sank in and Dominic struggled to grasp their concept. This had to be a dream…didn't it? "The world around us is such a big and scary place, with dangers and wonders around every corner," raved Miss Hawthorne. "And we can educate our pupils to the wonders of our planet through communication, geography, environmental studies…and so forth." She waved her hands excitedly as she spoke. "However, we do not usually cater to my own species." Her hands finally came together close to her chest, and she looked down at Dominic on the bed, smiling sadly at him as she moved slightly to reveal behind her a small, but powerfully built monkey dressed in a simple blue tunic. "May I present your nurse?" she said. "Sister Gemini Cana."

"You may refer to me as Sister or Nurse, whichever you prefer," she said simply as she pushed past Miss Hawthorne and sat on the bed by Dominic's arm and regarded the boy curiously. "I am not used to Human physiognomy," she confessed. "His brain may be damaged," she added as she peered close to him. Dominic examined her as she examined him and he could see the thick grey soft, close-curled fur which covered her body protruding from her clothing along her face, arms, and legs which ran across the knuckles of her hands. Her beady brown eyes danced over his face as they stared straight through him and his gaze met hers as she touched his hand gingerly. "He does appear to have many similarities to our own genii," she said as she reached for an apple from the bowl of fruit and berries on the bench behind her.

"I'm confident in your abilities Gemini, you have never let us down in the past," said Miss Hawthorne as she stood watching. Dominic could see her long thick tail twitch, and she hauled herself over the room with her powerful muscles to a small locker where she removed a bag from the container. She took a bite of the apple and Dominic could see her prime white teeth as they sank into the soft flesh of the fruit, then she dropped the apple into the bag and gripped at the metal bars which hung from the ceiling. Using her arms and tail, she swung back to the bed and perched herself by Dominic, peering at him through her piercing brown eyes. She removed the apple and took another bite, then removed a small metal object from the bag and placed it against her ear, then gently pulled at Dominic's clothing and placed the circular end against his chest.

"His breathing seems a bit erratic," she commented looking at Miss Hawthorne. "Is this normal in humans?"

"With everything he's going through, I expect it is," said Miss Hawthorne.

"How do you feel?" asked the nurse and Dominic frowned at her with a confused expression playing over his face. "I'm sorry…do you not understand? He may have brain damage or loss of hearing." He struggled to place her accent as she spoke to him, and he thought the broken English sounded Spanish or something similar. "Can you hear me?" asked Sister Cana slowly as she looked toward Miss Hawthorne who nodded in response to her question and spoke to the confused boy.

"Please Dominic," said Miss Hawthorne. "Don't be rude, if someone asks you a question it is manners to reply."

"I…I…don't understand," was all Dominic could muster in response.

"What don't you understand?" asked Nurse Cana.

"I mean," he looked at the monkey treating him, then to Miss Hawthorne, then Mr. Hindle and back again. "I don't wish to be rude…but how can I understand you?" His words were directed at Sister Cana, but he spoke directly to Miss Hawthorne.

"Oh, I see," she laughed and smiled at him. "Sister Cana is from Central America," she explained. "Her accent is from a region close to the border of Brazil," she smiled as though that had told him everything he needed to know.

"No…no…no," said Dominic frustrated that he had been misunderstood. "I mean…she's a monkey," he looked at her briefly. "How can I understand her, I mean how can she speak?"

"Ah…well…Mr. Hindle," Miss Hawthorne looked at her partner, who stepped forward.

"You see Dominic, each of our pupils and staff all wear a small collar which enables speech translation. As the vocal cords of each animal vibrate, the soundwaves are modified into variable patterns which are translated through modulated rings and capricious tones that are designed to evaluate a degree of coordinated resonance which is then translated into varying degree words and sounds which we understand." He smiled and clapped his hands together, "Simple really." Dominic still didn't understand, but he looked at the grey woolly monkey and peered at her uniform, specifically her collar. Her stubby grey fingers pulled down the material around her neck to reveal a small silver collar with a flat black square at the front of the device.

"I have done all I can here," said Sister Cana abruptly. "The patient is either stupid or…he is fine." As she spoke, Dominic could see small lights flash on and off on the collar with each word. She took another bite of her apple and turned to Miss Hawthorne, "I would suggest he returns to normal activity immediately." Dominic could hear the Latin American tinge to her voice as she spoke and looked toward Miss Hawthorne.

"I think it would probably be wise to address his living arrangements during his stay first…give him time to acclimatize to his current…position," she struggled to find the words as she looked at Mr. Hindle.

"Very well, my dear," he replied. "Grant."

The figure at the back of the room stepped forward and grunted its derision toward Dominic, and for the first time, he could see who the mysterious fourth 'person'...was. It moved slowly at first, with its arms pressed down against the floor, its fingers curled into tightly bunched fists which pressed against the cold floor of the nurse's office. Its large bulk offered a degree of power, and its long shaggy fur waved in the slight breeze from the window. It stood to its full height for a moment and stared down at the boy. Dominic could see the thick black fur which covered the body of the great ape run across its entire torso covering every part of the animal barring its face, hands, feet, and chest. He looked at the gorilla bearing down slowly on him and pulled back slightly fearful of the creature.

"Follow," it grunted in a deep African voice and moved out into the hall. Dominic glanced at Miss Hawthorne, who simply smiled at him.

"Grant is our personal assistant...and your group mentor. Any worries or problems, please don't hesitate to go to him," she pointed down the corridor at the hulk of an animal waiting patiently. "He'll show you everything you need." Dominic looked at the figure of Grant standing in the hall, filling up the light from the streaming window at the far end of the passage, and sighed.

"Follow," it called again, then stood on its hind legs and hammered against his chest and hooted at the small boy. "Come!" he commanded and turned and stalked down the corridor. Dominic climbed from the bed and with a final glance at Miss Hawthorne and Mr. Hindle took his first resigned steps into the school behind the gorilla.

Chapter Ten

GRANTED

Dominic followed at a distance behind the gorilla as they walked along the hallways of the school. He could feel the eyes of the 'pupils' peering out of their respective rooms as he passed each door. He regarded the large form ahead of him and marveled at the bulk of the animal squashed into the prim black suit, with its neat white shirt and tidy black bow tie. It occasionally glanced back at him and grunted as he walked along the wooden flooring on his feet and knuckles. "This way," he groaned in a deep voice, and Dominic shivered at the power in his voice. He still didn't understand the explanation that he had been given by Mr. Hindle, but found he couldn't question it…I mean, how could he? Here he was walking down a hallway toward a steep set of stairs, behind a talking gorilla, so the science had to be real…didn't it?

"Where are we going?" he asked in a meek voice as they stopped at the base of stairs. Grant simply turned and looked at Dominic and stepped on the first step and grunted derision in his direction. "Excuse me…" began Dominic again.

"Up," instructed Grant, not looking back at the boy.

"Yes, but where to?" asked Dominic patiently.

"Your room," grunted the gorilla and moved up the stairs without pausing or waiting for Dominic.

"My bag…"

"Up," snapped Grant in a loud voice, which caused Dominic to swallow his question and follow the ape up the narrow stair. His eyes drifted over the paintings which covered the walls as they walked and he wondered over the majesty of the pictures. As he passed by, he saw canvasses filled with scenes of jungles, splashes of colour and exquisite sites. "Home…" the words were softer in tone, and Dominic realised almost shocked that they had come from the gorilla ahead of him, who had stopped to stare at a vast image of greenery. He looked at Dominic and pushed his knuckle close to the image on the staircase, and Dominic slowly stopped by his side and stared at the painting.

"Where you come from?" asked Dominic cautiously.

Grant nodded slightly, "Home." His eyes never strayed from the painting as his fingers uncurled and ran down the canvas.

"Where…where is it?" asked Dominic gazing at the large ape.

"Africa," the tone of the voice was softer, almost genteel in nature. Grant turned his head slightly and looked at Dominic, and for the first time, the small boy could see warmth and depth in the ape that he had not seen before. "East Africa," he looked away from the painting and stared up the stair. "We go," he grunted and moved away without looking back. Dominic cast a final glance at the picture hanging on the wall and followed to the top of the stair in silence where he found Grant waiting patiently for him. As the boy reached the gorilla, the ape towered over his small body and indicated down the hallway. "Your room," he said and moved off down the passage. Dominic glanced back down the stair, then followed Grant along the corridor with new feelings for the animal welling up inside him. The gorilla pushed at a small wooden door…or at least it seemed small compared to Grant and Dominic pushed his way past the ape and into the room. He stood for a moment in the center of the room and gazed about at the meagre furnishing. A window was draped at the far end of the room which overlooked the expanse of the grounds beyond the building. On the table, which sat beneath the window sat a small plastic lamp and a bowl of fruit and berries similar to the one in the nurse's office. Three drawers were set into the desk's frame, each with a single brass knob handle. Set neatly under the tabletop was a singular wooden chair. He noticed that rails were set into the ceiling…obviously, the room had been designed for a primate rather than him. He looked at the hastily built bed, again catered especially for him he supposed. He could see vines and branches beneath the mattress, and his bag sat primly on the bedding. A simple woollen rug sat on the floor beneath his feet, and he spun slowly on his heels at his new home.

"Thank you," was all he could think of saying as Grant moved into the room and over to the desk.

He shoved at the paper on the surface with his thick stubby dark fingers and looked at Dominic. "Your timetable," he grunted and pushed the paper across the smooth wooden surface. "Read."

Dominic nodded and watched as the gorilla walked slowly toward the door. "Grant…" he said softly, then waited for the gorilla to stop and turn. "What happened…I mean, your home…how did you end up here?"

"Man," he replied simply. "I remember my home. My family group when I was young, we would sit together in the warmth of the shadows of the mountains," he bared his teeth in a parody of a smile as he spoke. "We would eat roots and bark and ants and laugh, then at night, we would sleep on the floor while my mother and sisters would climb into the trees. Then man came…he had bang bang sticks," he looked away from Dominic. "Man took me and locked me in box…took mother and killed father. Man, came, killed."

"I'm sorry," whispered Dominic, immediately regretting his question.

"Not your fault...man. Miss Hawthorne's father saved me and brought me here, and I am grateful, but I miss home..." he turned and moved out of the room pulling the door behind him. "I go, but will return soon." Dominic stood alone in the semi-gloom of the room and gazed at his feet. He felt a pang of pity for Grant and at that moment, saw him not as a gorilla, but as an individual and felt a pang of sympathy for him. He looked at the piece of paper on the desk and reached for it. Holding it in his hand while still standing in the middle of the floor, he cast his eyes over the paper.

"Biology...Communication...Physical Education..." he murmured to himself as he read the words printed in bold, italic letters across the paper. "Environmental Studies...Food Technology... Faeces Studies..." he frowned at that last lesson and wondered whether the words were right. His attention was drawn to the door where from the other side he could hear shuffling, and from beneath the door, he could see shadows of figures dance across the light. He drew his attention back to the paper in his hands and continued to read the subject line, "Behaviour and Social Study... Geography." The noise behind the door continued, and he wondered whether Grant had returned, he had said he would hadn't he, but somehow, he knew it wasn't him. "Is there anybody there?" he called out at the closed door cautiously and waited for an answer. He fidgeted nervously with the paper as he waited for a reply, which never came. "Hello?" he called again...still nothing. Dominic swallowed and moved closer to the door reaching out slowly for the handle...

Chapter Eleven
TOP DOG MONKEY

The door was thrust open before Dominic could touch the handle and in through the open doorframe, three figures forced their way into the room. The two largest figures placed themselves close to Dominic, one on each side of his body and Dominic glanced at both individuals in turn. They were both gorillas, smaller in stature than Grant, but nevertheless still larger than himself and still as imposing as the adult male. The first and largest of the apes stood on his right-hand side and wore a simple white t-shirt with a red letter 'M' outlined by a thin yellow and blue border on the front of the shirt. This ape wore no trousers and Dominic could make out a light silver tinge spreading down his back toward and mingling with the black fur which ran over his hind legs. The second ape was smaller in height and size and Dominic guessed was younger in age due to his physique. This one too wore a simple white t-shirt, with red arms adorning the material which stretched over its muscular arms. Dominic could see from the patches of fur which ran along the animal's arms that it was shorter than that of Grant and decided in his own head that if Grant was an eastern gorilla, then these two individuals must be from the west coast of Africa.

"Who are you?" demanded Dominic, trying his best not to show fear in his voice.

"Be quiet!" snapped a voice from the door. Dominic turned to the third figure and stared into its malevolent eyes. This third figure was smaller than its companions and indeed stood at the same height as Dominic when on its hind legs. It had a prominent red nose which protruded from the animal's head along a long thin snout and either side of the appendage ran a series of bony blue flanges which formed an impressive facial display which was completed by a small yellow tinged beard which covered its chin and ran around its neck forming a crescent of colour about its collar. Dominic could make out short speckled, olive-grey fur running across the animal's head and down its back and arms. Unlike the two gorillas, this animal wore a buttoned white shirt with a slight frilled floral decoration around the collar. A thin blue tie hung loosely around its chest and fell absently to the floor as the animal settled onto all fours and walked further into the room. It regarded Dominic through small beady brown eyes and grinned a tooth filled grin which sent shivers down Dominic's back. With the approach of the monkey, Dominic could see that it had a short stumpy tail which sat across a curvaceous mauve-blue rump. As it stood before Dominic, it stood on its hind legs again, raising to Dominic's eyeline and smiled at him showing Dominic at close quarters its fearsome pointed teeth, with four large fangs set into its mouth. "So…you're the new boy" it almost spat its words out as it spoke, while regarding Dominic with its cruel eyes. Dominic could only muster a slight nod to the creature. "Can't speak?" queried the animal grinning. The smaller of the gorillas grabbed at Dominic's arms while the other thrust its fingers into his mouth and forced his jaw open, whilst making sounds Dominic could only presume was laughter. "Oh yes, there's your tongue…for now," commented the animal before him. The two apes released their grip on Dominic and erupted in a series of hoots, beating their chests, and leaping up and down.

"What do you want?" coughed Dominic as he backed toward the rear of the room.

"What I want is you not to be here," spat the monkey, jabbing its finger harshly against Dominic's chest. "But since that cannot be arranged, what I want is for you to know who's in charge around here." He stood once again and bared his teeth before Dominic and casually ran his tongue over the front fang. "The name's Blue," said the mandrill and leaned in close to Dominic's face. "Don't forget it." Dominic could feel the hot breath against his cheek as the monkey spoke and the smell of its rancid breath invaded his nostrils and turned his stomach. It turned and spoke over its shoulder, "Michigan...Dakota." The two gorillas pressed against Dominic and stared down at the boy between them and grinned.

"Problem..." a deep voice erupted through the room and swept over the four 'pupils' in the room.

Blue looked up at the imposing form of Grant as he bore down on the students. "No sir, just saying hello to the new boy," lied Blue sweetly.

"Leave," instructed Grant as he stepped into the room, and watched as Blue sulked away, then moved to one side to allow Dakota, the smaller of the two apes to follow. He turned and saw the larger of the apes staring down at Dominic and spoke quietly in an audible whisper. "Michigan..." The older of the two apes ignored the instruction and continued to stare down at Dominic, pressing his face close to the boy's. It snorted loudly in his face and pushed his knuckle roughly into Dominic's chest, forcing Dominic back across the room and into the desk. Grant pulled himself to his full height and hooted its derision toward the youthful ape, beating his chest with his cupped hands.

Michigan lowered his body from Grant's bulk and almost

crawled past the ape in resolute submission. "Alright...alright... I'm going," he said as he walked past on all fours. He joined his comrades outside the room and looked back in briefly, before moving away down the corridor, moving in single file with Blue at the head of the parade.

Grant turned from the three individuals and looked back at Dominic who stood against the desk shaking. "You alright?" he asked. Dominic nodded and pushed himself from the desk and sat heavily on the bed.

"You came back," stated Dominic dumbly.

"I've brought you something...something to help..." said Grant. Dominic stared at Grant for a minute, then peered behind the ape as something moved...something small.

Chapter Twelve

A FIVER FOR DOMINIC

G rant moved slightly in the doorframe, and Dominic looked past the great ape and out into the hallway. Something moved behind the gorilla, then seemed to disappear in a blur of activity.

"What is it?" Dominic asked.

"Not what…who?" corrected Grant and looked behind him. He grunted and shuffled around, his eyes searching the empty corridor. Dominic watched as Grant's head turned left then right, still wondering what…no…who he had brought for him, and what did he mean by the phrase "to help him?" Grant looked up at the ceiling and grunted. "Down!" he barked and pointed his large stubby fingers to the floor. Dominic gazed upward, but his vision of the ceiling outside his room was blocked from his view. A muffled sound from outside the room and behind the ape signified whatever was on the ceiling had come down and was now behind Grant, who turned back to Dominic. "Fiver," he stated simply, and from his back, a small head poked around the large suited body.

"Hello," said the small individual. Even from this vantage point, Dominic knew this newcomer was a chimpanzee. He had seen enough of them in zoos and television to know what they looked like, even under the black and white baseball cap which sat on his head. His eyes were bright and sparkled with mischievous intent as he gazed into the room at Dominic.

"Hi," said Dominic cautiously, his thoughts still drifted back to the brief encounter with Blue and the two gorillas, and he knew this was not going to be an easy ride.

"He help," said Grant and moved silently down the hall away from the children.

Fiver stood in the doorway for a moment, cocking his head from side to side regarding the new pupil. Like his previous visitors, he wore a plain white t-shirt, with blue lines running along the top of the shoulders, but unlike the others, Fiver wore a pair of grey shorts which ran down his legs to his bare feet. "Err…come in," said Dominic eventually.

"ThoughtyoudneveraskitsfreezingouthereimFiverbythewayandivebeenaskedtohelpyousettleinasyourownmentorsotospeak i'llhelpyouwithwhattodoandwhatnottodoandshowyouaroundthatsortofthing," he smiled and leapt up onto the bed and whooped with joy as he bounced under his own weight pressing down against the soft springs in the mattress. "Whoahthisisgreatwhatisitwhyisitsobouncy?" he whooped as he bounced up and down on the bed, laughing with joy. "Ilovethisigottagetonewhodoihavetotalktotogetone?"

Dominic blinked at the newcomer, confused. He had acknowledged he had spoken to him but hadn't understood a single word he had said and wondered whether the collar thing was working. "Dominic," he said dumbly placing his hands upon his chest.

"Hahayourfunny," laughed Fiver, still bouncing furiously on the bed. "YourDominic," he leapt from the bed and landed close to Dominic and inspected him closely, pulling at his jacket and placing his hands inside his pockets. "Whatsthematterdonttalkmuchdoyou?"

"I'm sorry, but I don't understand anything you've just said," admitted Dominic.

Fiver stepped back from Dominic for a moment and stared at the boy up and down, causing Dominic to step back. The small chimp took a deep breath and sighed. "I am sorry," he said slowly and carefully. "Sometimes I get too excited and can have a habit of talking too fast," he admitted, before jumping back onto the bed. "I love this," he laughed as he bounced high again. "What is it?"

"Don't you have a bed?" asked Dominic.

"This is a bed!" whooped Fiver. "This is great!" He bounced high to the ceiling and grasped at the bars high above Dominic's head, hanging by one hand and one foot while laughing at the boy below him. "Let's start again...I'm Fiver," he said, stretching his hand out toward Dominic. "I'm your counselor."

"What do you mean?" asked Dominic.

"I'm sorry," said Fiver dropping to the floor and crouching close to Dominic. "Is that not the word...counselor...tutor... ward..." he waved his arms high above his head in frustration, then slapped them down against the floor. "I don't know," he called. "These words are confusing," he stood on his hind legs and looked into Dominic's eyes. "I'm here to show you around and get you used to the school," he slapped Dominic's back and jumped nimbly up onto the desk. "Stick with me Dom, and you'll be al-right." He picked up the paper which sat on the desk and scanned the lessons.

Dominic crossed to the desk and joined Fiver looking at the timetable. "Are you in my class?" he asked.

"Yeah," Fiver admitted and looked at the boy. "That's why I've been asked to show you around."

"Have you been here long?"

"First year," admitted Fiver. "You'll love Mr. Catta...he's physical education... and Mr. Bonobo," he paused and looked at Dominic, then his hands. "Does your species throw its own poo?"

he asked.

"No," said Dominic with disgust.

"Oh…okay, so you won't like Mr. Bonobo then," he said smiling. "And old De Brazza can go on a bit…he's biology."

"What's it like here?" asked Dominic.

"It's alright," said Fiver slowly. "Takes a bit of getting used to."

"What, like being away from your family?"

Fiver nodded, "nicechange," he said quickly. "Sorry…nice change," he corrected himself quickly.

"Where are you from?"

"Lincoln Park, Chicago," replied Fiver. "But my grandparents originally came from Central Africa. I don't know much about them or where they came from, that's why I was sent here in the first place" he looked out of the window as he spoke. "This is nearest I've been to freedom and the wild."

"Wouldn't you want to get out?" asked Dominic. "You know, leave and go to the wild."

"Whywhatwouldbethepoint?" said Fiver quickly. "The zoo is the only place I know…it's where my mother and father are. Why would I want to go anywhere else?"

Dominic felt uncomfortable and watched as Fiver stared out over the grounds of the school. He felt the small primate was not being completely honest with him. "Banana," he said eventually, pushing the bowl forward toward the small primate.

"Can't," said Fiver looking down at the bowl. "I'm allergic… banana intolerance."

Dominic laughed hard at the statement and Fiver stared at the funny noise which came out of the small boy, then slowly became aware that he was beginning to hoot along with him. The two boys laughed together for a moment before Dominic climbed onto the bed and laughed as he bounced on the soft mattress and held out his hands for Fiver to join him. The ape stared at him for a moment, smiling, then leapt from the desk and bounced on the soft mattress, bouncing higher and higher.

Chapter Thirteen
NEW BOY IN SCHOOL

The hall was packed with a multitude of eager faces. Dominic sat near the back with Fiver close to him and glanced around at some of his fellow students. He could feel their eyes on him; some hostile, others curious. He shuffled awkwardly in his chair and looked toward Fiver who nodded at him and smiled. This made him feel slightly better, but still, he could see the figure of Blue and his two friends at the far end of the hall. A chatter spread across the room from the various species and from his vantage point Dominic noticed that most of the groups sat in bunches together. The chimpanzees sat close to him, the gorillas sat toward the back of the hall, the tamarin's sat near to the front together and so forth. A hush descended over the hall as the large form of Grant strode confidently onto the stage at the front of the pupils. He looked out over the sea of faces and took his seat close to the middle of the wooden structure. Mr. Hindle shuffled onto the stage actively talking to an elderly looking orangutan. Dominic could see the old ape move slowly across the stage, leaning on the arm of the deputy and a crooked stick in his other hand. They were soon joined by a chimpanzee, a lemur, and a gibbon who all took their seats behind the front three chairs. Mr. Hindle helped the old orangutan into his chair and sat on the front row, looking over at Grant and nodding at the great ape.

Everyone waited patiently as more teachers walked across the stage and once all the seats were taken, Miss Hawthorne strode purposely across the stage and stood at the head of the teaching staff at a tall wooden lectern. "Good morning children," she spoke loudly and directly out into the auditorium.

"Good morning Miss Hawthorne," came the chorus of response.

"I hope everybody has had a good night's sleep," she smiled at the children in the hall. "Today we have a busy day ahead of us." Dominic could see as he looked around him, that she had the attention of every set of eyes in the room and more importantly held their attention and respect. "As we grow we learn," she spoke. "And as we learn we become aware of the world around us and our effect on those closest to us and all creatures we influence. From the deepest parts of Borneo to the metropolitan suburb of New York and everything in-between, our lives are important... at least to us, and our dreams fly with our thoughts. Hold your dreams tight with you, and there is nothing you cannot achieve. Keep your loved ones close and build your dreams around them. Through learning, we achieve the potential of what we can achieve not only as a species but as individuals. In learning we learn the true meaning of right and wrong, we learn there is good and bad in all species, and we become better individuals." She looked across the sea of expectancy. "Each of you...every single one, from the smallest aye-aye to the largest gorilla, all hold the key to your own enlightenment and spiritual release." She turned and looked at her colleagues, "We expect the same level of respect that we afford you, and with understanding, we can all prosper." She leaned forward on the wooden lectern and turned her attention back to the children. "Now...most of you have heard the rumours about the new pupil, and I am here to tell you that…yes, for the first time in the history of Hazeldene School we have accepted a child from the Homo-sapien genii…Dominic…Dominic Atwell." She looked out into the vast sea as she called out for Dominic. "Please stand," she called.

Dominic paused as the faces around him turned to look at him, and reluctantly he rose slowly from his seat. "Ah, there you are," said Miss Hawthorne. "Now I know most of you in the school have not had any dealings which this species…apart from myself and Mr. Hindle, but please do not be afraid of him or treat him any differently from any other student." She looked out over toward Dominic. "You can sit down now," she said softly. "As with any other child within this establishment, we do not tolerate any form of bullying or exclusion from any social standing within this school." Her tone softened as she continued, "Now then…you have twenty minutes before your first class, so I expect you all to prepare and be on time." She turned and glided from the stage and one by one each of the teachers rose to follow her, except for Grant who moved to the main doors and oversaw the tidal wave of children as they rose from the seats and moved in a single file from the hall.

"I've got something for you to look at before we go to class," whispered Fiver as they stood in line. Dominic nodded and followed his new friend from the hall and out into a large seated area outside the main building. He could see seats and benches spread out across the courtyard and various small groups had splintered off into small factions, while others had left for lessons early. Fiver placed himself down on a bench with a table and dropped his satchel on the wooden surface. He pulled at the buckles on the material and opened the bag and pulled a large book from within. Three other monkeys…no apes… sat with them and looked at Dominic.

"So, this is him then," said a large chimpanzee. Dominic looked at him as he sat and noticed that his face was darker in complexion and he seemed bigger than Fiver.

"He's cool, Bran," said Fiver, and he opened the pages of the book and looked at Dominic. "This is Brannigan," he said indicating at the larger chimp. "Penny…" he nodded to another chimp who had sat next to Fiver. She wore a pink dress, which spread out at the bottom with a deep white frill. He could see a subtle blue tinge in her eyes and realised that she was wearing make-up on her eyes. A pink bow in her hair made up her look, and she smiled at Dominic briefly before turning her attention to Fiver and moving close to him, who in turn pushed down the bench closer to Dominic. "Cooper," continued Fiver, as he nodded across the table to a small golden tamarin perched on a branch over-hanging the bench. "He's really smart," he confided in a whisper. "If you need help, he's your monkey," he winked as he spoke.

Dominic nodded and looked at the little monkey in the tree. The tamarin was small in stature but still larger than any other of the same genii that Dominic had seen so far. Its golden fur ringed its entire body, and unlike the chimps, this wore no clothing allowing his golden fur to dance in the slight breeze. Its deep brown eyes shone out of its grey face, and its head moved from side to side nervously as they sat in the sun. "I heard that, but I do have to concede to your logic." He said, not looking at Fiver.

"What's this?" asked Dominic looking at the book on the table.

"Cooper helped me with it," explained Fiver. "It basicallytellsyouwhattodoandwhatnottodo."

"Sorry," blinked Dominic.

"What my ignorant friend is trying to say is…this book is a reference to the basic social standings within our institute. A guide to what to do and what not to do…and also who to avoid," commented Cooper in a hushed tone, as he glanced over at the far end of the courtyard where Blue was sitting staring at their table. "Must go," chirped Cooper and dashed off the tree and across the courtyard. "See you in class," he called over his shoulder.

"We'd better go as well," stated Brannigan, glancing in Cooper's direction. "First class is old man Trethorne," he stood and rested his knuckles on the table. "Fiver…Five!" he snapped as the small chimp ignored his first request.

"I'm listening," smiled Fiver and stood, casting another glance across the courtyard toward another table.

"Stop mooning over her, way out of your league," commented Brannigan smiling.

"Cheap!" spat Penny, looking toward a table of baboons. Dominic followed their eye line and looked at the seated monkeys. Four baboons sat around the table, all with thick olive fur which covered their exposed bodies from beneath their clothing. One of the baboons stood and walked away from the table with a swagger in her walk and Fiver stared as her hips moved beneath her tight leather black skirt, revealing a curvaceous reddening rump. Like Blue, she had a long snout, but unlike the mandrill, this monkey's snout was a dark grey in colour which ran toward a dark face and small beady eyes beneath her heavy brow. Dominic felt himself grin as he could see a line of thin red lipstick skirt across the monkey's lips. He looked back at Fiver who seemed transfixed by the baboon.

"Who is that?" he asked.

"Cheap harlot…just look at her," spat Penny, again following their view. "With her cheap make-up and tight clothes…who does she think she is?"

"She's Kiki J, and she's gorgeous," whispered Fiver gazing across the courtyard.

"Humph!" grunted Penny and rounded on the small chimp. "She's not interested!" she snapped and stormed off in the direction that Cooper had gone.

"Somebody doesn't seem happy," commented Dominic watching Penny as she ran off on all fours over the lawn.

"She'll be fine," said Fiver, still looking over toward the baboon. "We'd better be off as well," he said turning to Dominic. "First class...Environmental Studies." He said, slapping the boy on the back. He laughed and sped over the lawn behind his friends. "Hurry up, don't want to be late!" he called.

Dominic turned and looked back at the baboon, who was standing looking directly at him and behind her, slowly moving with his two gorillas in tow, walked the imposing figure of Blue...

Chapter Fourteen
TREESY LEARNING

Dominic followed his new friends to a squat building behind the main hall. The dull grey brickwork was offset at intervals by green framed windows. Dominic was stunned at how plain the building looked and more importantly how similar it looked compared to every other school he had attended. As he walked into the building, photographs of students adorned the walls. Dominic paused for the briefest of moments as more students filed past him as he looked at the images of the pupils on the wall. He scanned each photo one at a time and saw in each various forms of apes and monkeys standing to smile, each with either a certificate or badge, while beside them stood Miss Hawthorne and a teacher. Again, Dominic was struck by the similarities between this school and his normal schools. The foyer walls were lined with pictures of trees and forests, and in the corner, a hand-made tree stood proudly displaying various forms of paper-mâché fruit, berries, and nut varieties from around the world. He could see pineapples mixed with bananas and kiwi, while small red berries hung with coconuts and acorns.

As he gazed at the imagery, he felt a sharp push in the middle of his back, and he stumbled forward against the wall. "Whoops," purred Blue. "I guess I didn't see you there flesh-bag," he hooped as he spoke and stood over the prostrate form of Dominic who had slumped to the floor. He stared up defiantly and frowned at the mandrill dressed in a neat white shirt.

"I'm not scared of you," Dominic said rubbing his arm as he sat on the floor.

"Big words for such a little boy," smirked Blue, revealing his large sharp front teeth. The two gorillas stood behind him and hooted with laughter as they watched the mandrill as he reached for Dominic.

"Come on babe…leave him alone," said a soft voice from the door. Blue paused with his hand hovering over Dominic's head.

"I suppose," he said slowly and carefully, not leaving his gaze from Dominic's. "After all, you never know what he's carrying." He stood to his full height on his hind legs and adjusted his red tie. "Come on boys, don't want to be late for class." He took one final glance down at the heap of Dominic on the floor and whispered, "Your girlfriend ain't gonna be around to save you next time." Then he walked on all fours down the hall to an open door near the rear of the building.

"I'm sorry," said the soft voice again. "You have to forgive his manners." Dominic turned his attention to the source of the voice and stared at the soft dark complexion of the baboon that Fiver had been obsessed with earlier.

"That's okay," he said softly and pulled himself slowly to his feet, then looked at her again. At this distance, he could see a deep intensity in her eyes as they sparkled in the hall lights and looked over the soft olive brown fur.

"Don't get the wrong idea," she warned. "I'm not interested in you, it's just that I live in a large group back home and have seen far too much of that behaviour from my own brothers."

"Oh, no," Dominic blushed at her words. "I just…well…you

are…"

"I know," Kiki J said smiling softly and winking at him, before moving off down the hall toward the classroom leaving Dominic alone with his thoughts. He turned and stared at the images of the forest spreading across the walls once again and sighed at their wonder.

"Beautiful, isn't it?" remarked a wistful voice from behind him.

Dominic spun around sharply in surprise, he hadn't heard anybody else walk in. "I'm sorry," he blurted out as he looked down at the ageing form of the large orangutan beside him.

"I said its beautiful," the ape remarked.

Dominic nodded sagely and looked back at the pictures of a high tree line. "Yes…yes, it is," he agreed, before looking back at this newcomer.

"You must be Dominic," he smiled slightly as he looked the boy up and down. Dominic studied him as he, in turn, was studied. It stood at the same height as Dominic, but the boy could see large swollen cheek pads which gorged over the ape's face, obscuring its eyes under a veil of wispy orange fur. A thick ranging ginger moustache and beard ringed a long thin-lipped mouth and covered an overhanging throat pouch. The animal's long arms stretched from its bloated body and Dominic could see that the arms were exceptionally large for a creature of its size. It held a crumpled wooden stick in its thick hands, its stubby fingers curling around the end of the cane and held it before its body to support his ageing frame. The ginger hair draped at length over his body, seeping across its bloated stomach and as he moved it swayed over its back resembling a long cape. "I'm Mr. Trethorne, your environmental teacher," he said simply. "And I would suggest we get a move on. Class is about to begin." He smiled and walked slowly down the hall, leaning heavily on his walking stick. The old orangutan spoke as they walked together, "In my class young Dominic, you will learn of the world around us and the effects your species is having on most of the species here at the school."

"So…I'm not going to be very popular," stated Dominic.

Mr. Trethorne laughed, and Dominic watched as the throat pouch beneath wobbled. "Not all of your species are inconsiderate, young Mr. Atwell. As you will probably find out during your stay here, every culture has its bad apples, and not everyone is rotten."

"I beg your pardon sir," said Dominic cautiously.

"Yes, my boy," said Mr. Trethorne, stopping and leaning on his cane once more.

"But…I didn't see many of your species at the assembly."

"No…no, you didn't my boy," confirmed Mr. Trethorne. "In general, we are a reclusive species and tend to live our lives in the canopy, alone. There are others of my kind here, we just like our own company…unless we are eating." He smiled and nodded at the classroom. "As you will see, the school is made up of all kinds. Now if you will," he waved forward, and Dominic stepped into the classroom and gazed around the large room.

Small desks and chairs sat in rows, while at the front of the class stood a large desk with a large blackboard covering the back wall. He could see Cooper, the small tamarin sitting at the front of the class with several other smaller monkeys chattering around him. The larger apes like gorillas sat toward the rear with chimps, baboons, gibbons and other of similar size spanning across the center of the room. A sudden hush descended over the chattering classroom as Dominic and Mr. Trethorne stepped over the threshold into the room. "If you could take a seat," said Mr. Trethorne as he moved slowly toward the front of the classroom. Dominic scanned the room and saw an empty seat in the middle of the class, with Blue in the chair behind.

The mandrill smirked and reached forward over his desk and

pulling the chair back he said softly, "I've saved you a seat."

"That's very good of you," remarked Mr. Trethorne as he settled at the front of the students and stared at Dominic. "If you don't mind." He waved his elongated arm toward the empty chair. Reluctantly Dominic moved through the rows of desks and settled into the empty chair, glancing toward Fiver who sat close to the window.

"Now, then children," said Mr. Trethorne turning and facing the board, reaching for a small piece of chalk. "We shall begin," he began to write on the black surface. "Where did we get to last time?" he asked in general. Cooper chirruped at the front of the class with a flurry of O's as he sat with his hand raised high above his head. "Yes, Cooper," said Mr. Trethorne without turning.

"We were looking at the effects of deforestation in the wild," said Cooper, turning to his neighbour and smirking.

"Yes…" said the orangutan slowly, turning to the face the class. "Now, before we go any further, I must stress that the actions of a species should not influence the behaviour of a single individual, do I make myself clear."

"Yes, sir," chorused the class.

"Blue," said Mr. Trethorne, looking toward the rear of the room.

"Yes sir," said the mandrill reluctantly.

"Very good, now," he turned back to the board and wrote some more words on the surface of the wall. "What do we know about deforestation?" He looked around the class at the sea of faces as they all stared toward the front of the class. Only Cooper sat with his arm in the air. "Anyone else?" asked Mr. Trethorne, before looking at the small golden tamarin. "Go ahead," he conceded.

"Deforestation is the systematic clearing of forest and rainforest areas to create wood products for man resulting in heavy loss of habitation for many different species." Cooper sat smugly staring about him as he answered the question, and then continued. "However, not all forms of deforestation are caused by mankind. There are different types caused by fire or natural grazing of indigenous species." He sat straight in his chair and folded his arms before him on the wooden desk and smiled at the teacher.

"Yes…well, quite right lad," reassured Mr. Trethorne and looked over the class. "Books out please and start making notes." He looked around at the students and then at Dominic. It would be difficult, he thought to himself, to make the topic sound fair against the threats posed by the human species. "The biggest threat to deforestation is man…" he paused and looked at Dominic as he spoke. "Large areas of land are systematically cleared at a rate of around twenty-nine thousand square miles per year." He was conscious that some of the students, particularly the ones from South America glanced toward Dominic. "Any ideas for the reason? Anyone but Cooper," he asked, looking at the small Tamarin as he spoke.

"Food…" hazarded Fiver.

"Homes," spoke a small lemur at the front of the room.

"Their animals," said a Macaque. "That's what is happening in Borneo and Sulawesi."

"Fun," spat Blue as he slumped back in his chair.

"Now, now Blue…and in response to the other suggestions… yes." He looked at the children and took his seat, leaning forward in his chair. "Mankind has a desire for a paper called money. This is what drives man, and unfortunately, this drive makes him dangerous." He rubbed his eyes as he spoke. "Our homes…the trees… are a major reason for mankind to make its money…whether it's the paper that they pulp from the tree itself or clearing space for agriculture and farming."

"What's agriculture?" asked Brannigan.

"Agriculture is the process that mankind uses to grow their

own products," explained the great ape. "But it has a cost." He sighed and stood, turning to the board, and making letters across the surface. "Farming, homes, money, expansion of their concrete jungles, paper, all contribute to the clearance of great expanses of forest each year." He wrote the words as he spoke them, then turned again. "Can anyone tell me the negative effects this has on the environment?" he asked and looked around the room at the expectant faces. Only Cooper sat with his hand in the air. "Cooper," he said softly.

"Loss of habitat for many species means a great decline in a species number which could lead to extinction."

A gasp from some of the girls in the class disrupted Cooper, and Mr. Trethorne looked out sternly at the children. "Children," he warned and looked back at Cooper.

"I believe that nearly seventy percent of animals currently habitat within these areas," commented Cooper as he continued talking. "And deforestation would make it difficult for many species to adapt to the new environment around them."

"Yes, Cooper," agreed Mr. Trethorne. "But what other effects apart from that can we expect?" he asked as he looked around the room. "Forest soil is mostly…" he paused looking for one of his students to come up with the answer for him.

"Dirty…" offered Fiver laughing.

Mr. Trethorne sighed, "No, Fiver. Moist." He looked around the room and wrote the word on the board, underlining it. "With no canopy covering, the forest floor would dry out leading to barren areas of potential desert areas. With no covering, the ground would become dry and arid since the canopy protects the ground from the effects of the sun the ground remains moist and fertile. Also, with no trees to generate a perpetual water cycle by returning vapor, there is nothing to fulfil this role if the rate continues. With no protecting canopy and protection from the sun, areas would become affected by extreme heat harmful to plant life as well as animal life," he concluded. "Anything else…Dominic?"

All eyes swung to Dominic as he asked the boy the direct question. He swallowed and stood to his feet unsure what to do or what to say, "Global warming," he offered meekly.

"Quite right!" exclaimed Mr. Trethorne. "Trees generally absorb the deadly gases which are causing the effect your kind call the 'greenhouse effect.' Without the trees, the increase in gases would speed up the build of deadly gas released into the atmosphere." He turned back to the board and wrote again on the surface with the chalk. "I want examples of deforestation around the world and the effects of that area, then for additional work, I would like possible solutions to the problem."

Dominic hovered by his desk and became aware that he was still standing. He lowered himself down into his chair, ignoring the noises of Blue and his cronies behind him. As he lowered himself down, he suddenly realised that the chair had been moved by the mandrill, and Dominic crashed to the floor, falling in a heap of arms and legs by the feet of Blue, who stared down at him with the back of Dominic's chair in his hand. A symphony of noise erupted as Dominic crashed to the floor with the echo of Blue laughing in his ear.

"Children," chided Mr. Trethorne, turning sharply from the board. "Children!" he snapped. "Settle down!" Some of the smaller monkeys had leaped onto their desks and were currently bouncing up and down, while others swayed from side to side clapping. "I said quiet!" shouted Mr. Trethorne as he used his long arms to haul his bulk onto the top of his desk. "In all my years of teaching…" he snapped and looked about the classroom as calm quickly washed over the children. "Mr. Atwell," he said slowly looking down the aisle at the boy, lying amidst a pile of wood from the chair and desk. "Is there a problem?" he asked.

Dominic looked at Blue, and the mandrill grinned a toothy grin at the boy. "No, sir," he said eventually.

"Just as I thought," snapped Mr. Trethorne. "Get to your feet immediately!" he roared, watching as Dominic pulled himself to his feet and stared at his feet. "Never, in all my years have I witnessed such disruption on a pupil's first day," he fumed. "What do you have to say for yourself?"

Dominic stood still staring at his feet and said nothing. "Please sir," the voice came from the desk behind him, and Dominic looked up at Blue who sat smiling with his hand in the air. Could it be? Could he really be admitting what had happened...that he had pulled the chair away from him?

"Yes, Blue," said Mr. Trethorne.

"Sir, when you turned your back, Dominic climbed onto the desk and began to pull faces at you, then he fell off the edge of the desk."

"Is this true?" said Mr. Trethorne. Dominic shook his head furiously but remained silent.

"Anyone?"

"Yes sir," the deep voice came from the back of the class and Dominic glanced around as the large form of Michigan stood by his chair. "He was making fun of you sir," he said smirking and lowered his large body back down slowly.

"No, I didn't," stammered Dominic, looking about the classroom. "Fiver...Brannigan...Cooper...you know I didn't," he said desperately.

"Please, Mr. Atwell," said Mr. Trethorne sadly. "I had wanted to hope for something better from your kind!" he admitted. "But alas, it seems my basic kindness has gone unrewarded." He slammed his hand down sharply on the desk, "Miss Hawthorne's office. Now!"

Dominic sighed and collected his things and moved out of

the class. Glancing back at Fiver, Dominic shook his head and pulled the door closed gazing through the glass into the room. Blue looked directly at him and pointed his curled fingers in his direction, then Dominic turned and lowered his head as he slowly walked down the hall.

Chapter Fifteen
T is for Teacher, R for Respect

Dominic sat in a large chair in the office of Miss Hawthorne and looked about the room as his thoughts wandered back to the events that had only just happened a few minutes ago, in the classroom of Mr. Trethorne the environmental studies teacher. Sitting in a headmaster's office was nothing new to Dominic, but this was different. This would be the first time he was in trouble for something he hadn't done. He fidgeted with his hands as he sat shaking his head in disappointment, not only with his own situation, but also that of his new so-called friends. Fiver had just sat and watched and said nothing. That hurt, but not as much as the lesson itself. He had known that the lesson would harm his reputation, but hearing Mr. Trethorne talking about the damage caused by mankind's influence hurt him deeply. He shook his head and thought about the size of the devastation caused each year by deforestation. That would be the size of a small country, he thought. His thoughts then strayed to his father and his business. He had made his fortune in the building line, and Dominic wondered how many trees had been cut down to build houses and what was the impact caused by that.

"Dominic," the soft voice came from the door, causing Dominic to break his train of thought and turn to look at the newcomer. Miss Hawthorne stood framed in the open doorway with Mr. Hindle and standing behind the two principles stood the forms of Grant and Mr. Trethorne. He hadn't heard the door open, and he turned away from the accusing eyes. "Dominic," Miss Hawthorne repeated gently as she walked across the floor and took her place behind the large desk in the center of her room. Mr. Hindle walked to the opposite side of the table, and took his place behind her, standing by the large bay window. The two apes stood toward the rear of the room and observed the scene in dormant silence for the time being. "Is everything alright?" Miss Hawthorne asked, leaning forward across the table and placing her hands on the wooden surface, entwining her fingers together in a cat's cradle of digits.

"Yes, Miss Hawthorne," replied Dominic quietly.

"Please Dominic, we are here to help," she said gently. "Now, I am going to ask again. Is everything alright?" Dominic refrained from answering, simply nodded his head in her direction, avoiding her eye-line. Miss Hawthorne sighed. "Dominic," she said, her tone changing and becoming harsher. "There has been an incident involving yourself in your first class," she said calmly looking at the old orangutan who had moved to the ornate fireplace. "We have witnesses stating you openly mocked Mr. Trethorne here and ridiculed his teaching," she indicated toward the teacher as she spoke. "Is this true?" Dominic remained silent and looked at his hands. "Please Dominic, is this true?"

Again, Dominic refused to answer, just stared at his hands, and avoided the eye contact of all in the room. "Dominic," said Mr. Hindle, "we only want to help you and your education, but we can only do that if you tell us the truth."

"The statement we have comes from a very dubious source at best," stated Miss Hawthorne. Dominic looked up from his contemplation and looked at the headmistress and listened to her words. "We have had problems with Blue and his known associates in the past," she was careful to choose her words as she spoke. "If you are having any problems…"

"No Miss," lied Dominic.

"Are you sure?" she asked again. Dominic nodded, and she looked at Grant, who moved forward and took his place by the chair that Dominic sat in. "Grant," she said.

"Last night," the great ape started, his voice a loud whisper, "you had trouble. I saw…"

"Dominic?" queried Miss Hawthorne. Dominic shook his head and returned his gaze to his hands once again.

"Please, Grant continue. What did you see?"

"Blue, Michigan, and Dakota in boy's room," said the great ape in broken English. "They threaten. I saw, I stop."

"Is this true?" asked Miss Hawthorne. Dominic nodded but still said nothing. "And what about today?" Her question was met with a wall of silence, and she instead turned to Mr. Trethorne. "Ebenezer," she said, and the ageing ape moved slowly from the fireplace and close to the desk. "Can you please tell me the events leading up to the incident, mainly what you told me outside?"

"Certainly, Miss Hawthorne," said the old ape. Mr. Trethorne leaned heavily on the small wooden stick in his hands and leaned close to Dominic's head. He gently reached out one of his long arms and placed his hand softly beneath the boy's chin, raising his head to look into his eyes. Dominic could feel the rough skin of the teacher's fingers caress his face as his head was gently raised. He looked into the dark eyes of Mr. Trethorne and saw years of wisdom in them, but also a warmth and compassion which he had not expected. "I saw what had happened in the hall child," he said gently, smiling at Dominic.

"I don't know what you mean," said Dominic.

"My species spends most of its life in the canopy of Borneo, son," he said in response. "The block that my classroom is in is the Borneo building, and that is why most of the ceiling has a re-creation of the canopy in my homeland." As he spoke, Dominic realised that while he had looked at the images spreading across the walls and the paper-mâché vegetation he had not looked up at the ceiling. "I spend a lot of my time in that canopy. As I said, we are a reclusive species by nature, and I do enjoy spending time there," he laughed at the expression on the boy's face. "I may look old, but I can still climb. I saw the altercation between yourself and Blue before class," he explained. "I saw the push..." he trailed off as he allowed the words to sink in. "Now, son, did Blue cause you to fall in class?"

"I can't say," said Dominic carefully. He could feel the tears building in his eyes as he struggled to understand what was hap-pening. Every school he had ever attended, he had been treated with hostility, but here...here it was different. They were kind. They were listening to him, all he had to say was...he couldn't.

"It's alright," said Mr. Trethorne softly and looked at Miss Hawthorne.

"If you're being bullied," said Miss Hawthorne, rising from her seat.

"It's not that Miss, I just can't," stammered Dominic.

"Please, understand this Dominic. While we are your teachers, we are also here to be your guides when you finally graduate. Our goal is to make all who come to Hazeldene to become better indi-viduals. To this end, I...we, need to create an environment where every student does not fear retribution from another child. We are the teachers, and while we promote a degree of learning, we re-quire a level of respect from everyone within the school, whether they be human or primate. Do you understand?"

"Please Miss," said Dominic softly. Miss Hawthorne nodded, and Dominic continued, "This is my first day, and it is hard enough as the only boy in school, but if I tell tales on a fellow student on my first day, then I will push everyone away. No one will trust me."

"Dominic," started Miss Hawthorne, but her words died in her throat as Mr. Hindle placed a hand on her arm.

"Let the boy speak," he said and looked at Dominic.

"With lessons like Mr. Trethorne's that damn humanity...and not through any fault of you, sir," he added hastily. "I enjoyed your lesson, but a lot of the animals here have all felt man's cruelty at some point, and I have to bear that. So, please, I cannot admit to the treatment of Blue or his friends."

"I understand," said Miss Hawthorne eventually. "While I don't agree with your actions, I do understand your motives. A lot of the classes will be like Mr. Trethorne's and do not show humanity in a good light, and you will probably find hostility until the other students accept you. And so, while I do not condone your actions, I must commend your attitude." She sat in her seat and looked at her colleagues. "What is your next class?"

"Communication," Dominic replied.

"Well, at least that should be more fun for you," she said. "You are dismissed."

"Am I being punished?" asked Dominic.

"For now...no," said Miss Hawthorne. "But, please do not place yourself in a position that could lead you into trouble. Do I make myself clear?"

"Yes, Miss Hawthorne," Dominic stood and walked to the door.

"Dominic," called Miss Hawthorne as he reached out for the door handle. He turned and looked at the four figures in the room. "If you have any problems, my door is always open."

"Thank you," he said softly and pulled the heavy wooden door and moved out of the room, leaving the adults in the office.

"Gentlemen," said Miss Hawthorne as she straightened her

pencil thin skirt and turned to stare out of the window. "I think we will need to keep a close eye on our Mr. Atwell for his own safety, don't you?"

"And Blue?" asked Mr. Hindle.

"We say nothing," she said. "His father was the same when he came here, and look how he turned out. We must offer all the students the same level of education, regardless of their stature." She turned and faced the three other adults in the room. "Now then, if we could go about our business. And thank you all for your time." As Mr. Hindle and the two apes left the room, Miss Hawthorne turned and faced the window again, staring over the expanse of the grounds and sighing heavily. "Father," she said softly, "give me the strength…"

Chapter Sixteen

NATURE CALLS

Dominic walked in silence along the winding path as he walked from Miss Hawthorne's office in the main building to another of the outlying buildings in the school grounds. He still felt frustrated at what had happened, and he felt a betrayal of trust from Fiver and his friends, but also considered the influence of Blue. Someone would have to stand up to this...could he say, boy? He pondered the thought as he stopped by a post and looked at the signs pointing in different directions. He pulled his timetable from his pocket and consulted the small pamphlet, then looked back at the signpost, studying the various metal arrows pointing in different directions. He glanced again at the paper in his hand and read the words sprawled across the page. "Communication class, Mr. Sericules Reddington...Amazon block," he mumbled, and turned his attention again to the sign and read the pointing arrows. "Borneo..." he said under his breath and looked up and across the gravel path toward the low-level building where he had spent the first lesson. "Madagascar...Congo...Gibraltar," he spoke each word in turn and briefly looked up at the path as it meandered through the overgrowing greenery.

As he was looking across the recreation area, he could see the familiar forms of Fiver and Brannigan walking on all fours toward a large glass framed building. He consulted his timetable again and set off after the two apes as they headed for a group of primates gathering outside the block. He could feel a mixture of anger and disappointment grow in the pit of the stomach as he watched Fiver as he stood on his hind legs and began talking to another ape that Dominic did not recognize. He still couldn't believe that this chimp had failed to stand up for him in the class and wondered whether he would do the same in his position.

"Hello friend," chirped a small voice above Dominic's head and the boy paused mid-step to look up into the over-hanging trees. His eyes scanned the leaves, and he squinted as the sun poked through the branches and locked onto a patch of golden fur.

"Oh, hi Cooper," he said eventually.

"Doesn't sound too much like you're pleased to see me," squeaked the small monkey indignantly.

"I'm sorry…it's just, what happened in the class," he felt ashamed of his words even before he spoke them and felt his face blush as he faced the tamarin.

"I understand," said Cooper softly, moving along the branch toward the boy as his face contorted into a soft smile. "You have to understand Dominic, that there is a hierarchy in the school and Blue, well…he's kind of the one at the top of the tree, so to speak." Cooper glanced around at even the sound of the mandrill's name.

"But he's a bully!" exclaimed Dominic.

"It doesn't matter," said Cooper. "When you've got muscle like those two in your pocket, you can pretty much do whatever you want. Don't blame Fiver for what he did, any one of us would have done the same."

"Can't you stand up to him, if all of you…"

"It's no good," interrupted Cooper. "We know our place."

"You're scared."

Cooper nodded, "Yes, if you like," he admitted. "We're scared, but nevertheless we're safe."

"So, that's it then," spat Dominic. "He throws his weight around and gets his thugs to push you about, and you all fall behind him like…like…sheep."

"You don't understand, it's Blue…" apologized Cooper.

"Maybe I don't understand, but I do know if we all stood together and stood up for ourselves, no-one would live in fear of Blue or his mates." Dominic shook his head as the pupils by the building began to move in through the doors. "No-one should live like that," he said. "We should go. Otherwise, we'll be late." The small tamarin nodded and leapt from the branch and perched itself on Dominic's shoulder, wrapping his snaking tail gently around his neck. Dominic could feel the warmth of his body as it pressed against his shoulder as the fur pushed through the material of his own cotton shirt. Tiny hands pressed hard against the front of his chest as Dominic ran along the gravel path and as he moved he realized that the small monkey was quiet.

He looked at the building as it loomed over the horizon and he considered it as the stones crunched beneath his feet. The building stood in two distinct parts with a small squat formed building similar in height and stature to the Borneo block. As with the Environmental block, small decorated windows adorned the outside of the building, and a large double door beckoned them in. He could trace ivy sneaking up the outer walls of the building as the creepers ran and played across the pebble-dashed exterior. The other part of the building was far larger in construction, with its main bulk rising far above the smaller part of the building. He happened to glance around him as he slowed to a walk and realized that this was the largest building within the school grounds, apart from the main house itself. Massive metal beams ran like a spider web across the glass-domed frame, and Dominic traced two panels of glass as they ran across the surface of the building to the ground. A massive glass dome...or bowl, he thought as he stood on the threshold of the building. Through the glass, he could see the interior of the building was ringed by a line of trees which spanned the windows. Despite the foliage inside, he could make out a large circular area in the centre of the building and wondered what the area was used for.

"What's this lesson like?" asked Dominic as they walked into the building and stalked down the hall.

"I hate it," said Cooper eventually, breaking his silence.

"Why?"

"All that shouting and screaming, I can't handle it," admitted Cooper.

"I don't understand."

"Communications," enforced Cooper. "Surely you know. Talking."

"Oh, okay," said Dominic. "Like English."

"English?" queried Cooper.

"This must be the famous Dominic Atwell," came a loud voice from an open door. Ahead of them in the doorway stood a medium-sized monkey with a wash of red fur.

"Yes sir," Replied Dominic politely. The monkey regarded him briefly and forced its thin lips into a slightly wry smile.

"Very good," it said eventually and looked him up and down. "I've never been this close to a human before," he remarked. He continued thoughtfully, "Well...apart from Olivia and Eronymous, I mean not a human child...like yourself." He beckoned toward Dominic as he spoke and Dominic could see from his hand movements that the thick set monkey was becoming agitated. It swayed from side to side as they stood in the doorway uncomfortably for a moment before turning on his heels and walking on his thick fingers and feet into the building. Dominic followed and examined the monkey as it walked before him. The monkey had a swathe of thick red fur which covered the entirety of its body from its darker patches of maroon spreading across its head and face and down toward its long, thick tail. Dominic could see a dis-colourisation toward the animal's lower back as the fur became tinged with a ginger hue making the fur seem slightly golden in colour. From his position behind the monkey, he could see that his tail was pre-hensile with a thinning of fur on the underside of the appendage and Dominic realized this would be used for grasping and holding when the animal was in the wild.

"Excuse me, sir," spoke Dominic quietly as they came to a large set of double glass doors. He looked through the glass at the gathering of monkeys and apes within the large hall.

"I'm a red howler," said the teacher simply, looking at Dominic through its bright eyes.

"That wasn't what I was going to ask," Dominic replied.

"Go on..." nodded the red howler.

"English...I mean communications," his words trailed off while he watched the other pupils separating into small groups across the floor. "What is it? I mean, there are no chairs."

"Then I believe, Mr. Atwell, you may be in for a surprise," he held open the door for Dominic to enter the hall and stepped in behind him.

"Good Morning Mr. Reddington," chorused the class as they settled into small lines.

"Good Morning children...I hope you are all well," he walked into the middle of the hall and gazed around him on his hind legs, his fingers entwined behind his back. "Have you all been practis-ing?" he chuckled.

"Yes sir," they chorused again.

"I know you have," laughed Mr. Reddington. "All the other teachers have been complaining." He turned and looked at Cooper who was hiding behind Fiver's back. "Mr. Mane…" he said quietly and waited as Cooper pushed his way past the chimp. "Have you been practising?"

Cooper nodded his head slightly, then paused and shook his head, "No sir."

"And may I ask why?" The small tamarin stood silently and looked at the floor. "May I remind you, Cooper, that your grades may be excellent across the other lessons, but in this class, you are failing dismally."

"While I appreciate the complexities of your class sir, I believe my skills are more intellectual." Cooper stammered as he spoke, still staring at the floor.

"Please, Mr. Mane," said Mr. Reddington, softly staring down at the small monkey at his feet. "The lessons you will learn in my class may one day save your life." He dropped down onto all fours and circled the Tamarin as he spoke, looking toward Dominic. "The object of my class is not only to allow you to understand the process of communication, but the different syllables required to encourage, guide, mate and alert." He walked as he continued to talk until he stopped before a large wooden stage. Using his long flexing tail, he reached up toward the overhanging branches of the adorning trees within the glass-domed building. The tail snaked its way around the rough branch and hauled the monkey off the floor and onto the stage, while all the time he continued to talk. "The whole point of speech, whatever form, is to communicate. By using a series of defined processes and calls we can define a greater understanding of the world around us. Picture if you will…a starving family. Mothers and babies with no food…and yet here we have a tree full of fruit and berries. How do we tell them that they have food within distance?" He looked about him as he spoke. "Through distinctive calls. What if that same family is feeding and behind them…what is that? A lion? A tiger? How do we warn

102

them? This is the point of my lesson…to utilise our communica-tion skills to a greater point." He raised himself up on his hind legs and looked over the class and continued, "Now then, class…if you could line yourselves in an orderly fashion." He waved before the front of the stage and waited patiently as the children lined up before the wooden structure.

"Thisisgonnabegreat," whispered Fiver quickly as he sidled close to Dominic.

"No," whispered Dominic as he looked at the chimp beside him and slowly walked away down the line until he stopped close to a group of baboons.

"We should stop meeting like this," smiled Kiki J as she glanced sideways at Dominic. "People will talk," she giggled as she spoke.

"No, it's not like that," stammered Dominic, blushing a deep crimson.

"Is that how your species displays its attraction?" she asked.

"No…no…I…" he glanced away embarrassed as she laughed at him. He could see the solemn face of Fiver staring up the line and then looking away quickly, focusing instead on the teacher on the stage.

"Now we are ready," spoke Mr. Reddington. "Today we are going to establish a communication network through vocalized transmissions. In the wild, this training will strengthen your voice to travel great distances and warn others of impending danger." He drew himself up and placed his hands on his lower stomach. "You will need to draw in a deep lung full of air to pronounce the sound across greater distances," he explained, pressing down at the bottom of his diaphragm with his thick fingers. "The air will be forced up through your body from here," he said, pushing down beneath his rib cage. "And then pushed up through the diaphragm and abdominal cavity until it reaches the thoracic cavity. The re-sulting inhalation causes the external intercostal muscle between the rib cage to elevate, causing a longer and deeper exhalation of breath. This will result in an elevation within the thorax which forces the air to course through our body and escalates into a series of excitations within the bronchial tendon allowing the peripheral muscle to contract." Mr. Reddington smiled as he looked around the classroom filled with blank expressions. "Now…shall we give it a try? Take a deep breath and hold…" he breathed in and placed his hands on his stomach again, looking at the pupils in the room. "Then release…" he smiled as he spoke and took a deep breath, holding the air in his lungs for a moment before releasing in a deep, sharp whoop which echoed across the glass rafters of the ceiling. "Children," he said, looking at the class.

Dominic watched as each one of the apes and monkeys in the room copied the actions of the teacher, each with varying degrees of success. Some of the calls were loud and reaching, while others barely a squeak. He took several deep breaths and paused, glancing at the others surrounding him. He looked at the ceiling and stared for a moment at the glass panels high above his head and followed the trails of creepers and vines as they passed over the dome. Taking one final glance at Fiver, he shook his head and breathed deeply, then staring at the ceiling released his voice into the canopy above his head. He felt a joy sweep through his body that he had not felt in a long time as he howled at the ceiling. As he whooped he felt the breath escaping from his body in a series of calls, the hoots turned from deep resonance and into something resembling laughter…and for the first time in days…months… Dominic laughed.

Chapter Seventeen
RUMBLE IN THE JUNGLE

D ominic walked across the open foyer to the school canteen and for the first time in a long time felt content. The Communication class had been liberating and the feeling as he screamed all his pent-up anger felt as though a heavy weight had been lifted off his body. He paused outside the double doors and peered through into the dining area. He could see rows of tables littering the floor space of the canteen, with benches spread around the room pushed firmly beneath and beside the tables. Like most of the school, lavish vegetation decorated the vast open space and gave the opulence of an actual jungle environment. With small sitting areas designed into the canopy high in the rafters of the building, Dominic could understand why this building had been called the Jungle, with its garish display of flowering shrubs and towering trees which reached into the roof and stretched out their wooden appendages, brushing the steel craft-work with their leafy fingers.

"Welcome to the Jungle," snarled a raspy voice behind him as he stared into the room, and an accompanying thrust in the middle of his back sent him sprawling onto the uneven floor.

"Watch it!" snapped Dominic, rolling onto his back, and gazing up at the snarling, vicious form of Blue.

"Or what? You'll hit me with your soft pink skin?" The mandrill laughed and was joined in his chorus by the two gorillas who stood respectfully behind Blue. "Or will you go running to your girlfriend?" he mocked and stepped over the boy, pausing to scuff dirt into Dominic's face with a slight kick backwards. Dominic stood from the floor and gazed defiantly at the back of the mandrill as he walked through the canteen on all fours.

"Don't even…" commented the rough low voice of Michigan.

"Think about it," finished Dakota, his fellow ape and they two barged past the boy, ruffling his clothing and hair as they past.

Dominic stared down at his dirty uniform for a moment and sighed heavily, murmuring to himself, "apes."

"I wouldn't let anyone hear you talk like that darling," cooed Kiki J from the side of the hall. "It could be misconstrued as a threat."

"I'm sorry," whispered Dominic, straightening his clothing. "I didn't realise anyone else was here."

"Good job for you," she said, and she passed him into the canteen, her hand touching his shoulder and trailing across his chest. She winked at him and smiled, "I can work up quite an appetite." With that, she dropped to all fours and swayed across the floor of the canteen. Dominic watched her walk away for a moment, before following into the room.

He could hear Fiver's voice close by as he spoke quickly to the others with him, "Wow,justlookatherisn'tsheamazing. Justlookatherbuttockssoroundandred" the words were a blur, but even from this distance, Dominic knew he was still swooning over the baboon. He took a deep breath and picked his way across the floor, taking care not to trip on the various roots which snaked their way up from the floor or slip on the discarded leaves. He sniffed and wrinkled his nose as an unpleasant odour hit him and he tried to place what the smell was…rotting meat? Plants? Fruit? Wet hair?

No matter what he thought of, Dominic couldn't quite place the smell which offended his nostrils. Carefully picking his way across the room and trying not to breathe in any of the obnoxious air, Dominic found a long counter laden with food pressed up against the side of the hall. He tentatively picked up a flat wooden tray and walked along the rows of metal containers which housed varying food substances. He looked at the different tubs filled with apples, oranges, bananas, some fruit he didn't recognize, nuts and the bodies of insects and small amphibians. He made his way along the counter, peering at each container, in turn, carefully considering his choices.

"Excuse me," came a curt brisk female voice. Dominic looked up at the source of the voice. "Yes...you, excuse me." The voice came from the other side of the counter, and Dominic stared into the brown eyes of the small monkey. It had a soft brown coating of fur which covered all its body, but it was the animals face which held his attention. While its eyes were sharp and curious, its face was lined and wizened from time and its nose...its nose... Dominic stared at the nose of the monkey as it stretched over its face and widened into a flat, loose piece of flesh which hung over its snout and mouth. "You must be the boy...Dominic," she said, glancing from side to side as she spoke. Dominic fought his urge to laugh as the fleshy nose bounced across her cheeks as she moved. "You have a specialized dietary programme, designed to suit your culinary needs," she explained and pointed to a small cart, separate from the length of the counter. "All special needs children food is located in that area...if you please." She waved her tiny hand at the cart and Dominic as she spoke, "go on...go on."

Dominic moved slowly away from the counter, thinking what did she mean by "special needs"? He considered the words as he approached the small wooden structure which sat half covered in moss, dirt, and vines. He looked at the small cardboard boxes which sat perched within the vehicle and read along the lids until he came to a small container which proudly boasted 'Dominic Atwell' in felt tip pen on the lid. He took the container and placed it on his tray and moved away from the food, looking over the sea of faces for an empty seat. He could see Fiver waving furiously toward him, his grinning face beckoning him from the other side of the room. Dominic looked at his tray of food soulfully and shook his head, turning from the small chimp's gaze, and picked his way over to an empty table by the window. He could feel the disappointment in the chimp's gaze as it bore down into his back. Dominic toyed with the plastic lid, prizing it off the cardboard tray and stared at the contents. Two sausages, peas, and a plate of chips, with a pot of jelly at the side of the tray. He sighed and absently pushed small green balls around the plate.

"It's not easy is it, son," said an old voice from behind him. Dominic turned and looked at Mr. Trethorne as the old orangutan lowered himself from the canopy.

"Oh, hello sir," said Dominic politely. "I didn't see you there."

"Quite," replied Mr. Trethorne and settled himself on the bench by Dominic. "And what if you had?" Dominic shook his head and shrugged, returning his attention to the peas on his plate. The old ape regarded Dominic for a moment and watched him forlorn as he continued to play with his food. "I'm not your enemy son," he said softly. "Let me help."

"I don't need any help," said Dominic, still gazing at his food.

"We all need some kind of help son, and I think you do more than anyone else," said Mr. Trethorne, reaching across the table as he gently placed his hand on top of Dominic's. "It isn't easy, is it?" he repeated. "Being the odd one out?" He paused and smiled. "But then I think you always have been, haven't you?" Dominic stopped pushing his peas with his free hand and looked into the kind old eyes of the orangutan. "I'm guessing, every school you've ever been to, you've been the outsider, the outcast. But you've always survived, haven't you? How?" His eyes searched Dominic's face as he spoke. "I think, you've always relied on being the biggest...the loudest...the boldest, but here, here is different." Mr. Trethorne stopped talking and looked around the hall at the other primates as they ate and talked. "It's not nice being the one whose being pushed around, is it? How many have you done it to?" he queried as he followed Dominic's gaze to Blue and his friends. "That's you, isn't it?" he asked Dominic as he stopped at Blue and watched as the mandrill pushed a small lemur's food into its face to a round of laughter from everyone around them. "How many, Dominic?" whispered Mr. Trethorne. "How many?" He stood and removed his hand from Dominic's and smiled at the boy, "You're finally seeing the pain you've caused in others, aren't you, and it hurts." He turned his back and placed his hands on the sides of the tree and spoke into the bark. "It's never too late to change, Mr. Atwell. Just remember as you change, who your friends are." He glanced at the sad form of Fiver as he sat alone by the wall. Dominic followed his gaze and listened as the ape climbed the tree, while his eyes never left the sad face of the chimp. "You will need your friends," drifted the voice from above, "if you are to move onward."

Chapter Eighteen
NAKED AMBITION

Dominic walked from the Jungle and along the gravel path thinking about the words Mr. Trethorne had said to him. He had been right...Blue was him, or at least what he used to be. All of the schools he had ever been to, he had acted the same. His thoughts drifted to some of the schools he had been expelled from and the reasons behind his actions. He remembered Eastwood Academy where he had locked a boy in the girl's toilets until he had cried. He remembered the laughter from the other children and his own glee. He thought about Knight Templar Junior School where he had dropped a goldfish down the back of Susan Crimp's dress and again he could hear the laughter echo in his head as the children around him laughed and mocked as she screamed, writhed, and cried. Then there was Forest Walk, the school where he had pulled a chair from Emily Watkins as she went to sit and thought about his own experience at the hands of Blue in Mr. Trethorne's lesson. With a sudden realisation, he said to himself, "I'm no better than Blue!" He continued mumbling as he followed the path toward the large ominous Forest Gymnasium. His mind drifted to the events he had witnessed from the mandrill since he

had been here, not just to himself but to others as well. Sure, there
had been the intimidation in his room and the chair incident in
Environmental Studies, but he thought of the small monkey being
tortured in the Jungle Canteen with his own food. Then there were
all the little things that had been dismissed by most. The pushing,
tripping, and threats all amounted to one thing…Blue was a bully,
and by his own admission, Dominic was as well. At the time, he
hadn't realised his actions were hurting others, he only thought of
the laughter and the attention he was receiving at the time. "I can
change," he said determinedly, as he came to a stop and gazed at
the door to the building.

"I'm very glad to hear that, Mr. Atwell, I don't think I would
like to see you climb with all those clothes still on," came a high-
pitched voice from above his head.

Dominic jumped and gazed into the tree, but saw nothing.
"Hello?" he said cautiously, unsure whether he was being the butt
of another joke.

"Hurry up lad," came the voice. "You're late!" it snapped, then
from the tree dropped a small lemur, his eyes shone brightly in
the sunlight, and he stared at Dominic as he stood in front of the
building. "Come on, come on!" he clapped quickly as he spoke.
"I'm your Physical Education teacher," he explained. "Mr. Julian
Catta, and you're late!"

"Sorry sir," apologized Dominic looking at his map of the
school. "I think I lost my way."

"Not interested, Mr. Atwell. What I am interested in is you're
late, and my other students are waiting!" The small monkey fidgeted as he dropped onto all fours, his black and white ringed tail
snaking and curling in the air as though reaching for the sunlight.
Dominic moved slightly as Mr. Catta walked elegantly past him and
he was reminded of the way a cat moves, gracefully and delicate
on its feet. His brown-grey fur bristled in the sun, and he paused

to look at Dominic through his bright orange eyes which stared at the boy from its dark triangular eye-patch. "Come on then!" he snapped. Dominic started in action at the brusqueness of the teacher's words and hurried into the building.

The gymnasium was large and expansive, mostly decorated in the same fashion as the majority of the school...except while the other classrooms had tables and chairs, this was an open space. Trees and vines were mixed with other equipment for climbing, swinging, and crawling beneath. He stood and watched for a moment in awe as his fellow students were already working some of the equipment. He marvelled as chimps, lemurs, tamarins, gorillas, and others swung, leapt, and climbed with ease across the canopy and equipment, and then he looked at his own scrawny arms and wished the floor would swallow him up. "Go on," urged Mr. Catta. "Get involved."

"I'm not really dressed for it," stammered Dominic looking down at his own clothes.

"Don't worry," eased Mr. Catta. "We have some alternative clothing for you...I believe you call it a pee kit."

Dominic hid a smirk and nodded. "Sort of..." he murmured and stood waiting for the lemur to return from a side office that he had disappeared inside. He watched Blue as he pushed another pupil from a balancing beam to riotous laughter from his friends and nervous laughter from those around him. Was this how he had been viewed before he had come here? He asked himself as he watched the bully.

"Here, here," said Mr. Catta as he stopped by Dominic and handed him a pair of white shorts and a blue t-shirt. "Get changed and let's see what that hairless body of yours can do, shall we?"

"Where do I get changed?" asked Dominic, looking around for a changing room. Mr. Catta blinked at him and shrugged. "You know, take my clothes off?" continued Dominic blushing slightly.

Again Mr. Catta blinked at him and simply shrugged. "I can't get changed here," complained Dominic.

"Why not?" asked Mr. Catta

"It's...you know..." Mr. Catta shook his head. "It's embarrassing."

"Oh, don't worry," laughed Mr. Catta. "I won't be embarrassed, now please."

"Not you, me...I mean everyone will see..." he glanced down his body as he spoke.

"Now Mr. Atwell!" snapped Mr. Catta. "Enough of this attention seeking, get changed now and meet me by the climbing apparatus in five minutes!" he snapped and bounded off across the floor.

Dominic watched him go and suddenly became very self-aware of his body as he slowly unbuttoned his shirt and removed it. He felt very naked, even though he still had his trousers on and desperately covered his bare torso as he pulled the t-shirt over his head. He paused as his fingers hovered over the button at the top of his trousers and he snapped it open and pulled his trousers down and reached quickly for the shorts...

"Looking for these!" laughed a deep voice from behind him. Dominic whirled around and stared at Blue as he stood behind Dominic twirling the white shorts in his hand. Laughter sparked around the mandrill from the small crowd that had gathered around them.

"Give me those!" snapped Dominic as he stood in his tiny red underpants, his hands desperately trying to cover his body.

"Come and get them," laughed Blue as he tossed them from one hand to another.

"Please Blue," Dominic begged.

"Look at those disgusting hairless legs," Blue chided and laughed as he pointed at Dominic.

"Come on Blue, give me them," Dominic could feel himself getting upset and was resolved not to cry in front of the class.

"Get them yourself!" snapped Blue as he threw the shorts onto the lowest branch of a nearby tree and ran off laughing into the jungle simulated gym.

"Idiot," snivelled Dominic as he stood beneath the tree and gazed up into the branches. The shorts weren't high up, but far enough for Dominic to climb. He was acutely aware that he was standing half-naked in his red pants still surrounded by his class-mates, some of whom were staring, others were laughing. His attention was caught solely by the white clothing sitting just out of reach so that he wasn't aware of the giggling mandrill as he grasped at Dominic's underwear and pulled them down to his ankles before whooping away in joy. Dominic almost died with embarrassment and covered himself up with his hands, before bending down to pull up his underpants from his feet.

"So, that's what a human looks like," he could hear the voice of Kiki J as she spoke to her friends and giggled, as Dominic blushed even further.

"Dominic..." the sound of the voice and his name broke his embarrassment, and he looked up into the tree. Fiver sat on the bottom branch, a pair of shorts in his hand and he smiled down at the boy and lowered the clothing down to him.

"Thank you," whispered Dominic, avoiding his eye contact. He pulled his shorts over his legs and up over his pants and whispered into the tree. "Fiver..." but when he looked back at the branches, the small chimp had gone. Sadly, he searched the gym for signs of his friend, but couldn't find him through the trees.

"Mr. Atwell!" shouted Mr. Catta. "Could you please hurry, now that your little show is over."

Dominic opened his mouth to protest, but instead closed it and thought 'what would be the point?' He ran over to the teacher who was standing beneath a series of ropes. From the bushes, Blue stared at the boy through his small beady eyes and snarled. "Your time will come, boy," he said quietly, then disappeared back into the shrubbery...

Chapter Nineteen
MONKEY BARS...?

D ominic stood with Mr. Catta and looked at the apparatus before them. Apart from the natural equipment like the trees and vines, a series of man-made objects were scattered across the gym, most of which Dominic recognised. Fixed against the walls were a series of rungs and handles running up the length of the building up to the ceiling where the canopy swamped over the wooden appendages. Across the floor were hurdles, vault and other leaping types of equipment and swarming in the middle of the room sat a large climbing frame. The mixture of metal and wood framed the apparatus making it the prominent structure in the room. Dominic looked at ropes from high fixings in the canopy which snaked their way down to the floor. He sighed with trepidation at the various pieces of equipment.

"Right!" said Mr. Catta. "Let's see what you can do." He leapt over to a large piece of equipment with four wooden legs with a soft oblong cushion running along the frame. "You recognise the pommel horse?" asked Mr. Catta looking at Dominic, who nodded slowly at the lemur. "What I want you to do, is to run up to the horse and leap over it, placing your hands firmly in the centre of the equipment to help stabilise your body...is that clear?" He slapped the centre of the soft top of the horse as he spoke indicating the position he expected Dominic to place his hands.

Dominic nodded and looked around the floor at the base of the pommel horse. "Is there no springboard?" he asked looking over the rough strewn plant life which adorned the floor.

Mr. Catta laughed. "Why on Earth would we need anything of that type!" he exclaimed. "Look around your Mr. Atwell, every one of my students has pose and grace, and more importantly strong arm and leg muscles. Since you have no tail to assist your balance or climbing, then I must assume your muscles must compensate for your unfortunate deformity."

"I'm not sure…"

"Come on Mr. Atwell, get to it."

Dominic gulped and walked hesitantly away from the apparatus, then turned and looked at the equipment and sighed. "You can do this," he said to himself staring down at the horse. "You can do this," he repeated determinedly. "One run, leap, and it's done. You can do this."

"Come on Mr. Atwell!" called Mr. Catta and Dominic wished silently that the teacher would stop encouraging this way, as every time he did he drew a small crowd to watch. Taking a deep breath, he ran toward the ominous horse. He could feel the speed picking up in his legs as the air burst from his lungs, his face contorted into a determined grimace as he went faster and faster and nearer and nearer. He could do this…he thought, as the equipment got closer and closer. One sudden burst and it would be over, quicker, and quicker, closer, and closer…the air was bursting in his lungs, the breath was forced from his body. He could feel the eyes of the students pressed against him as the equipment drew into touching distance. His legs went quicker and faster, then left the floor…

He stared at the ceiling from his position on the floor, and he groaned as his chest ached with pain. "What happened?" he asked.

He could hear laughter around him as Mr. Catta leaned over his prone body and said, "You failed, Mr. Atwell, you failed." The teacher reached out a tiny hand toward the boy, "But you failed spectacularly." He smiled as Dominic accepted his hand and climbed to his feet, placing his free hand on the pommel horse which still stood silently next to him.

Dominic rubbed the growing pain in his chest and breathed heavily as he looked at the equipment, "I didn't do it then?" he queried.

"Hardly son, but you did give it a good go."

"What happened?"

"Imagine this…" said Mr. Catta smiling, holding up his hands. "This is you" he waved his left hand. "And this is the horse," he waved his right hand and swiftly brought them both together making a loud clapping noise. "Result…Now I think we have established that your leg muscles are relatively weak. So, I think…we should try something a little different." He looked around him as he spoke and smiled. He then dropped onto all fours and picked his way over the floor looking at various pieces of equipment before settling at a small framed apparatus. Either end of the equipment was framed with tall wooden legs and running from one end to the other were a series of bars connecting two long beams. "Let's see how strong your arm muscles are," stated Mr. Catta, standing beneath the equipment. "Are you familiar with these?"

"Monkey bars!" exclaimed Dominic. "I've used these before," he smiled as he spoke.

"I beg your pardon?" asked Mr. Catta, blinking at Dominic.

"Monkey bars," he said hesitantly.

"Or as we call them…climbing bars," snapped Mr. Catta.

"I didn't mean…" stammered Dominic. "It's just…well, I… kind of…"

"Just get on with it!" snapped the teacher. Dominic gulped and stood beneath the bars, looking up at the parallel rungs which ran along the beams. He could not see anything to climb to the bars and again had a sudden dread and attempted to leap to the rungs, falling a distance short of the bars. "Now what is it?" snapped Mr. Catta.

"I can't reach," admitted Dominic.

Mr. Catta sighed and rubbed his black triangular fur between his eyes with his tiny fingers and shouted over the growing crowd, "Dakota!" The crowd parted, and the large form of Blue's friend Dakota moved through the students. "Lift him up," groaned Mr. Catta. 'Why Him?' thought Dominic as he noted the teacher's sudden change in attitude after he had mentioned the monkey bars. Had he offended the teacher, surely that's what they were called? The gorilla stood in front of Dominic and grunted in his face, delivering a fine mist of snot and mucus over him. He smirked as the hot air from his mouth repelled Dominic and lowered his body to grip the boy's legs, lifting him high into the air. Dominic felt overwhelmed at the ease with which Dakota lifted his body, and he could feel pain in his legs as the gorilla squeezed them together. Dominic ignored the pain and, determined not to give the ape the pleasure of seeing his discomfort, he grasped at the bars above his head. His fingers curled around the wooden rungs and as Dakota released his grip, he found himself dangling in free air. "Let's see you swing over to the far side," said Mr. Catta coldly, as he walked over to the far end of the climbing frame.

Dominic looked over, his face cast in a determined frown, and then swung his legs to give him momentum. His body rocked back and forth as his legs moved inward and outward and he thrust his hand forward gripping the next bar. He sighed inwardly as his fingers curled around the bar and allowed the momentum of his body to propel him to the next bar. He continued this process over the next three bars before his fingers slipped from the wooden rung.

He felt a burning sensation in his shoulder as he struggled for breath, forcing lungfuls of air out of his mouth and into the gymnasium. With effort, he hauled his hand back onto the rung and hung limply over the gym floor before starting to swing his legs again. Another two rungs came and went, and Dominic could see he had almost completed half of the equipment. His face pulled into a snarl as he forced himself over another two rungs, before his hand slipped for a second time, but unlike before, his arm could bear the weight of his body no longer and with an unceremonious crash he tumbled to the floor, his back hitting the leaf covered gymnasium with a hard thud.

"Maybe, you should find what you are best at by yourself," said Mr. Catta, resignedly rubbing his eyes as he peered down at the boy. Dominic nodded and pulled himself up and peered around at the laughing faces which surrounded him again. Their ridicule made him more determined to find something that he could do. He'd show them, he thought, and spied the free-standing rope which fell from the tree above. He looked around him as the other students dispersed and went about their own business, leaving him by himself.

"I'll show them," he said and stamped across the gymnasium floor and gripped the bottom of the rope and stared up toward the canopy as the rope disappeared through the canopy. His chest throbbed with pain from the pommel horse, and his back ached from the fall from the climbing bars, but he was still determined to show that damned teacher he could do this. He rubbed his hands on his t-shirt and gripped the end of the rope, glancing up again before leaping off the floor. The rope bit into the hands as he hauled his body off the floor and, using his feet to support his body, forced himself up the rope. He moved slowly away from the ground, motivated by the laughter which still rang in his head and the pity he had received from the teacher. He would show them!

His movement was slow and careful as he placed one hand above the other, hauling his body slowly up the rope, and his feet stabilised his body weight as he continued his slow climb up the rope. The canopy was getting nearer, and Dominic risked a quick glance downward at the floor below. Even at this distance, he felt no fear at his height, just a fixed determination to prove everybody wrong. He pulled his body further up with his hands and could feel the burn of the rope beneath his hands, but his determination fuelled him forward.

"Knock, knock," came a silky deep voice from the nearby trees. He stopped and looked over as the face of the mandrill emerged from the bottom of the canopy and snarled at the boy.

"Leave me alone," spat Dominic and moved his hand above his other pulling him further up the rope.

"I don't intend on putting a hand on you," sneered Blue, and grasped the rope above Dominic's head savagely. He pushed his body weight against the rope, causing the line to buck violently. Dominic clung to the rope desperately as it swung in the air.

"Blue," he said desperately as he clung to the rope.

"Like I said," sneered the mandrill, "I won't lay a hand on you," and he pulled violently on the rope again.

As the rope moved under Blue's touch, Dominic fell...

Chapter Twenty
IMPATIENT PATIENT

Everything was dark, but he could hear voices echo in his head. He tried to move, but the pain that crossed his body kept him in a laying position and kept his eyes firmly closed. After a few seconds, he decided to stop trying to wake and instead listened to the voices which surrounded him.

He could hear Miss Hawthorne speaking, "So, no one saw anything."

"No Ma'am," replied Mr. Catta. "I've spoken to most of the children and each one has nothing to say. They either didn't see anything or don't know anything."

"I find this very hard to believe," replied Miss Hawthorne. "Somebody must have seen something."

"The last person to see anything was Blue, who stated after the incident on the climbing bars, Dominic went to the climbing ropes and began to ascend."

"Then what?"

Mr. Catta shrugged, "I'm sorry, but that was the end of Blue's statement. He claims to have left to work on some ground equipment, which has been confirmed by both Dakota and Michigan."

"And you believe them?" asked Miss Hawthorne.

"I've no reason not to," said Mr. Catta simply.

"This will not do," said Miss Hawthorne. "It simply will not do. The school is struggling financially, we cannot afford any kind of incident of this nature. If the family sues..." Dominic could hear her sigh and furniture move in the room and imagined her sitting. "How is he?" she enquired.

"There are no apparent breakages, only superficial cuts, and bruises across a lot of his body. I, however, cannot ascertain to his mental condition," the female voice was familiar, and it took a while for Dominic to place, eventually realising it was Nurse Cana speaking. "Until the subject has recovered his consciousness, I cannot determine his mental capacity."

"Mr. Catta, please," said Miss Hawthorne. "Can you please go through the events before and up to the accident."

"As I have stated before, Olivia, I had spent time with Dominic here, trying him on various apparatus, then left him to find his own physical peak and concentrate on the other students in my care. I was made aware of an incident by Cooper, who had seen the end of the accident."

"And can you just repeat his statement for me please."

"He heard a scream, looked up and saw Dominic falling from the climbing rope. I am sorry, Olivia, but I cannot add anything further."

"Yes...oh...thank you Julian," responded Miss Hawthorne. There was silence in the room for a moment, and Dominic listened to the footsteps as they walked across the floor. He heard the door open and close as he lay on the bed. "Eronymous, what are we going to do?" she asked softly.

"There's no point worrying about it, honey," said the calm voice of Mr. Hindle softly. "Whatever happens we'll handle it together."

Dominic felt a hand on his arm as Miss Hawthorne spoke

again, "Shall we contact the family?"

"Not just yet," said Mr. Hindle. "Let's give it a few hours and see what happens with Dominic here first."

"I suppose you're right," she conceded. Dominic shifted slightly on the bed and groaned. "Eronymous!" exclaimed Miss Hawthorne.

"Olivia," he responded and moved closer to the bed placing his hands on her shoulders. "Miss Cana, could you…" Dominic opened his eyes slightly and peered through the haze as the form of the woolly monkey leapt onto the bed by his body and rested her hand on his forehead, leaning close and staring into his eyes.

"He does appear to be coming around," she stated.

"Eronymous, could you inform Miss Nasilis to prepare some of the special soup we have brought in?" Mr. Hindle nodded and moved to the door, pausing to look back at the boy for a moment before smiling and disappearing into the hall beyond the room.

"His pupils seem a little dull," commented Miss Cana. "But I think he may be all right." She leapt from the bed and bound across the room to her desk where she snatched at a banana in the bowl. "A little potassium should build his strength."

"Please Nurse Cana, if I may have a moment alone with Dominic?" said Miss Hawthorne.

The woolly monkey paused for a moment, banana in hand, then nodded and replaced the fruit in the bowl. "Certainly, I'll be outside."

"Dominic," said Miss Hawthorne, sitting on the edge of the bed. "Can you talk?" she asked. Dominic nodded, he felt a pain course through his body as his muscles moved his neck and he winched. "Can you tell me what happened?"

Dominic thought…he remembered the monkey bars and the fall, he remembered the laughter at his expense, he remembered the rope and climbing up the free-standing object and then…he remembered Blue. He remembered as the mandrill grasped at the rope and pulled, he remembered the sneer flash across the ape's face as he jeered at Dominic as he desperately held onto the rope. He remembered the fall…the darkness…the pain. He felt anger rise through his body as he heard the laughter ring in his head. "No Miss," he said finally.

"Are you sure Dominic?" asked Miss Hawthorne. "Are you really sure no-one else was involved?"

"No Miss," lied Dominic. "I slipped and fell. It was my own fault." He closed his eyes and turned to face the wall.

"Quite," commented Miss Hawthorne. "Dominic…if anyone is bullying you…" she touched his arm.

"There was no-one else involved!" snapped Dominic. "Can I please get some rest."

"Certainly," said Miss Hawthorne uncertainly. "But, if you feel the need to talk…or remember anything differently, you know where to find me."

Chapter Twenty-One
SICK BED

Everything was dark, and as Dominic stirred from his sleep, he felt a slight panic rise through the pit of his stomach as he could hear voices but could see no faces. He had no idea whether it was night or day and with nothing to see he could make no sense of his surroundings. He struggled beneath the blankets of his bed and could hear a female voice whisper urgently to her unseen companions, "He's awake." He tried to force the blankets off his body and look around, but instead found himself surrounded by darkness and pinned beneath the pile of rough, itchy bedding. Panic grew and spread across his body and with a degree of urgency he struggled to sit, his arms flailing across his body as he forced the blankets off him. He remembered a time when he was at home with his parents and had complained to his mother that he couldn't get up for school because his duvet was too heavy, and now here he was in complete darkness and struggling beneath a pile of heavy blankets. The weight pressed down on both his body and heart as the memories of his time at Hazeldene surfaced in his head. The fall...Blue...Fiver, and the words of Mr. Trethorne. Dominic struggled to sit on his bed and swung his head around, desperately searching for someone...anyone, but still darkness swamped his eyesight.

"I...I can't see," he stammered quietly.

"Open your eyes," whispered the soft voice with the hint of a giggle. Dominic felt stupid almost immediately with the force of her words as he realised he still had his eyes firmly shut. He slowly opened his eyes and allowed the light of the room to invade his senses, and as his eyelids fluttered open, the figures blurred into view. He looked around the room and the children, and slowly he recognised the figures as they cleared in his view. Penny sat by his bedside and smiled warmly at him.

She raised a hand from her lap and waved at him. "Hi," she giggled. Dominic smiled slightly at her and turned his attention to the two figures standing behind her and recognised Brannigan and Cooper. He looked back at Penny, then followed her eyes to the end of the bed, where a small figure sat on a small metal chair asleep. Dominic looked back at Penny and toyed idly with his hands.

"How are you?" he asked awkwardly.

"We're fine," Penny replied. "You know, things just carry on." Dominic shrugged and sat further up in bed and looked down toward Fiver and the small monkey shifted in his chair. "He's been here every day since you came in," Penny said softly.

"How long's it been now?" asked Dominic.

"Three weeks...since the accident," said Penny.

"Accident," scoffed Dominic.

"Yes accident," snapped Penny, casting a swift glance toward Fiver, then back at Dominic. She repeated, "Three weeks...since the accident and we've just continued like nothing's happened while you've laid in this bed feeling sorry for yourself."

Dominic felt ashamed of himself as Penny's words stung him and he looked down at the one friend he had made in the school. He could see a few slight marks and decolourisation on the skin of the chimp and frowned, before turning back to Penny. "Those marks…"

"Blue," she said coldly and lowered her head.

"I don't understand."

Penny sighed, but the words struggled to form in her mouth, and instead, Brannigan spoke. "Blue was bragging in the yard about what he had done to the human boy," he explained. "He drew quite a crowd."

"Everyone was laughing," interrupted Cooper.

"Yes, thank you, Cooper," sighed Brannigan. "Yeah, well…he was saying how he taught you good and proper."

"What's this got to do with Fiver?"

"I'm coming to that," complained Brannigan. "Well…yes… Fiver told him to stop." Dominic looked down at Fiver, who still sat sleeping at the foot of the bed. "He strode over the yard and stood before Blue and told him to shut up."

"Why?" asked Dominic staring at the cuts across Fiver's face.

"Because he's your friend. Who knows why after how you've treated him, but he's still your friend. He stood before Blue and told him to stop…and well," Brannigan looked down toward the foot of the bed.

"He got beaten," concluded Dominic.

"That's one way of putting it," clapped Cooper. "Blue kicked him all over the yard. Hit and bit him…"

"What happened to Blue?"

"Nothing," said Penny sadly.

"What do you mean nothing?"

"Everyone told the teachers, Fiver fell out of a tree. Lost his footing."

"But surely…" started Dominic.

"But nothing," snapped Penny. "That's not the way it works," she said. "I don't know what happens in human schools, but here

Blue is the Alpha. What he says goes."

The small group sat in silence for a few minutes until Dominic's next question broke the silence, "Is this your first visit?" he asked eventually.

"Fiver's been here every day," admitted Penny. "He's been very careful and only came when you've been sleeping."

"I don't understand why he'd…"

"Because of you," snapped Penny. "You and your words. He didn't want to upset you by turning up when you've been awake so every day when you've slept, he's visited."

"I never knew," Dominic said softly.

Penny stood and quietly pushed the chair back and turned to the door, hopping across the floor to the large doors at the end of the room. She turned and stared accusingly back at Dominic in the bed. "I blame you," she said and pushed at the door and disappeared into the corridor beyond, followed by Brannigan and Cooper. Dominic sat upright in his bed alone with the sleeping figure and tried to make sense of the words that he had been given by the trio. His fault…he looked at the marks on Fiver's face and felt a pang of remorse for his inaction as much as his actions. His eyes strayed for a moment from the chimpanzee at the bottom of the bed and took stock of his surroundings which had been his home for the past few weeks. The walls were stark and bare, shining out a depressing drab whitewash across their surface. A few posters featuring medical images of apes and skeletons scattered around the room broke the waves of white. Through the flaking paintwork of the small window at the far end of the room, a steady stream of sunlight cast its shadow across the plain wooden floor. Dominic shook his head sadly and admitted to himself that he was hiding, not just from Blue but from his own admission. He had lied and hidden in this room from the world beyond the hospital bed. He was a bully, or at least he had been, and it had taken someone bigger and stronger to show him exactly what he was. The difference was, he could change. He was sure of it, absolutely sure.

"I can go," the small voice broke his train of thought and brought him back into the plain medical room. He looked down at the bottom of the bed and looked into the eyes of Fiver...his friend. The small chimp had stood and fidgeted awkwardly with his cap in his hands, folding the material between his fingers. Guilt swept over Dominic as he examined the face of Fiver and between the small cuts and abrasions which marked his face he could now see the swelling beneath the ape's left eye. Dominic shook his head, but no words came from his mouth as he continued to stare at Fiver as he turned the small cap over and over in his hands. Fiver stood unsure what to do as the two boys waited in silence for something...anything to happen between them. Dominic's eyes never left Fiver, while Fiver kept glancing toward the door, the floor, the walls...anywhere but at Dominic. "I should go," Fiver said eventually.

"No, please, stay," stammered Dominic. Fiver hovered, wanting to stay, but unsure whether he should. Slowly he took his seat and rested a hand on the bed, but still avoided eye contact. "I'm sorry..." whispered Dominic softly, almost as though the words died in his throat.

Fiver looked up and for the first time gazed into the eyes of Dominic. "Pardon," he said almost teasingly.

"I said, sorry," repeated Dominic. He looked pleadingly into Fiver's eyes. "What...what happened...what I said," he struggled to find the words as he leant forward, pushing the sheets from his body.

"They hurt...your words," said Fiver accusingly.

"I know," admitted Dominic. "It's just...I never...you know."

"No, I don't," said Fiver simply.

"What happened, and what I said, it's...well."

"This is a waste of time," snapped Fiver and stood from his chair, pushing the legs noisily back across the wooden floor.

"I am a bully," the words fell from Dominic's mouth, and his head fell into his chest, tears forcing their way out of his eyes and trailing down his cheeks.

"What!" said Fiver aghast.

"I am a bully, that's why I was sent here," Dominic continued as Fiver sat back down. "I went from one school to another, being expelled and excluded from class after class. I never realised what I was doing, I just remembered the laughter," his words were tinged with regret. "I never realised the pain I was inflicting on the children I picked on. I never saw it, I just knew the laughter." The admission gave Dominic a feeling of relief, but also regret. "When I look at Blue, I see me. I see what I was." He looked at Fiver and spoke, "I am ashamed of my actions, but it took someone like Blue to show me what I was. I look at you and see someone who is good, someone who cares for others, I want that. I want to be liked for who I am, not what I do. I need you to help me."

Fiver sat listening to Dominic's words and nodded, "Your words…"

"Please, I don't want to be like Blue. I don't want to be remembered as a bully," he held his hand out toward Fiver. "Can we start again? friends?" he asked cautiously.

Fiver stared at Dominic's hand for a moment, then smiled and gripped the boy's hand, "Friends…"

Chapter Twenty-Two
TIME FOR A CHANGE

"Were you really like Blue?" asked Fiver after a short while. Dominic nodded. "Yes, I was," he admitted. "But coming here has made me realise who I was and who I could be. Meeting you, Penny, Cooper, and Brannigan and seeing the actions of Blue and the effects on others has made me realise what an idiot I was."

"So, what now?"

Dominic looked around at the white walls as he spoke, "I think I should stop hiding here and get back out where everyone can see me."

"What about Blue?"

"Especially Blue," replied Dominic as he swung his legs off the edge of the bed and placed them on the cold floor. "He's been top of the tree for too long, I think it's time for a change, don't you?"

"Are you sure?" Fiver seemed uncertain, but Dominic nodded defiantly.

"Yes," he said firmly. "I should know better than anyone else. A bully is essentially a coward. He relies on fear to keep others quiet." He turned to Fiver and waved his hands furiously as he spoke. "You pick on the weak through physical acts or ridicule, while you keep the strong at bay through numbers." Dominic pulled his trousers on over his pyjama bottoms as he spoke. "The more people you have laughing with you, the greater your support and the harder it is for others to stand up to you." He pulled his t-shirt over his head, and his words became mumbled as he still continued excitedly, "You did it. You stood up to Blue."

"Yeah," mumbled Fiver, the back of his hand running down the side of his face. Although mainly healed, the cuts under his touch still stung at the memory. "And look what happened," he complained.

"But, what if everyone stood up to Blue!" said Dominic frantically. "We stand together."

"They won't," stated Fiver.

"What?"

"The children…they won't do it. They're scared."

"Why?" asked Dominic.

"I don't understand," admitted Fiver.

"Why are they scared?"

"You've seen Blue," said Fiver simply. "He's massive. He's strong and powerful, and he's got those teeth."

"Is that all?"

"Michigan and Dakota." Dominic frowned at the names and sat back on the bed.

"But we have the whole school," he said eventually.

"You'll never do it, the other mandrills…"

"The other mandrills are as scared of him as we are," interrupted Dominic from the bed. "But he's still only one person." He stood from the bed and walked to the door, pausing to look back at Fiver who was still hanging back by the bed. "When I was at home, my dad used to watch a lot of wildlife programmes on television. I never really took much notice, but what I do remember is every now, and then they would show hunters…lions, tigers, those sorts of things…and every so often the weaker animals would fight them off through their weight in numbers. Fiver, if we stand together, we are strong. We can stand up to Blue and his thugs."

"If you're sure…" trailed Fiver slowly.

"I'm not, but we have to try."

Fiver nodded. "What should we do?" he asked.

"First things first," said Dominic. "I need to get back to lessons and get noticed. If the other pupils see me make a stand against Blue, then hopefully they'll be more susceptible to helping us."

The night had been a restless one for Dominic. While his words to Fiver had been bold, he still could not help feeling slightly worried about his first encounter with Blue since the 'accident.' The other children didn't bother him, but as he dressed, he thought about his reactions and interaction with the mandrill. It was true what Fiver had said, he was bigger, stronger and more intimidating, but Dominic had to stand up to him and make a stand, not just for the school but for himself as well. He elected to miss breakfast, the feeling in his stomach pushed any thought of food from his mind and he slumped on his bed gazing at the window on the far side of the room. In contrast to the hospital bed, his room was exactly as he had left it, adorned with colourful pictures and maps. Fresh fruit had been placed in the bowl on his desk, and he briefly wondered whether this had been Grant or Miss Hawthorne. Clouds moved slowly across the sun as his room darkened to match his mood. A sharp knock at his door brought a deep sigh from Dominic and, resigned to the events ahead, he rose and crossed the floor of his room to the door. His feet made no sound on the carpet, and he could see the shadow beneath the door shift as the unseen person waited patiently. He gripped the door handle and pulled it open to reveal Fiver jumping from foot to foot.

"They'veheardyourback," he gibbered excitedly.

"Slow down," eased Dominic, laughing at his friend. "Who has?"

"The other children," enthused Fiver. "It's all over the school," he clapped his hands and bounced excitedly on the spot. "Comeoncomeonletsgo."

"Five, you're doing it again," sighed Dominic.

"Idontcarethewholeschoolistalkingaboutyoucomingbackto-class."

"Fiver, I didn't get any of that," complained Dominic.

"Don't care," laughed Fiver, a little more careful with his words. "Let's get to class," he gripped Dominic's hand and pulled him from the room and down the hall toward the staircase. "Everyoneswonderingwhatyoulldo."

"Fiver," snapped Dominic. "Slower."

Fiver stopped and stared at Dominic. "What will you do?" he asked looking at Dominic, searching his eyes for answers.

"Learn," said Dominic simply. "What lesson do we have?"

"Geography," said Fiver carefully.

"Then let's make sure we're first ones there," said Dominic smiling. "After all, we don't want to upset our teacher...or our audience."

Dominic sat at the front of the class and stared forward at the board which sat on the wall before him. He was acutely aware of the chatter of children behind him, but still, he kept his eyes on the front of the class. Fiver had chosen a desk next to Dominic's and whispered furiously, "Blue's giving you daggers." Dominic smiled at the news but remained staring toward the front of the class. Fiver looked around at the sea of faces behind them. He could see Blue at the back of the class, his fists clenched as they rested on the top of the wooden desk. Michigan and Dakota flanked the mandrill as usual, but for once most eyes were not focused on the ape but on the small, scrawny human sitting ignoring the mandrill at the front of the class. Dominic allowed his eyes to wander across the front of the classroom at the posters of Africa, Asia, and South America. Garish images of trees mixed with maps and mountains and Dominic marvelled at the geography presented on the posters, but then he smiled to himself. They were after all in geography.

"Good morning children," chirped a small voice from the back of the class as the door at the rear opened and closed. Dominic fought a great urge to turn to face the voice and see his teacher for the first time. "We shall carry on where we ended the last lesson on…can anyone remember where that was?" The small voice was growing as the figure picked its way through the maze of tables and chairs, then stopped next to Dominic's desk. "Mr. Atwell… Dominic," it said, and for the first-time Dominic allowed himself to turn his head to face his teacher. "It is a pleasure to meet you." Dominic looked down beside him at the small figure of his teacher as he stood by his desk. "Allow me to introduce myself, I am Mr. Tashiki Osorro, and I am your geography teacher." He smiled at Dominic, and in turn, Dominic smiled back.

"Thank you, sir," he said politely. Mr. Osorro was tiny and stretched his small body to reach the top of Dominic's desk to talk to him. As his hand rested on the top of the wooden surface, Dominic was struck by the impression his claws…not nails… made on the wood as his long spindly fingers spread over the table. His greying fur ran the expanse of his body and Dominic could see slight flecks of red running through the fur along the primates back and merging into its winding orange tail. Mr. Osorro leapt onto the desk and regarded Dominic through his bright brown eyes.

"I do hope you're feeling better after your most unfortunate accident," he said, his pink lips quivering beneath the wisps of white hair which sprouted from his chin, his head bowing slightly as he spoke respectfully to the boy.

"Yes sir, quite better," stated Dominic smiling.

"Good, good," said Mr. Osorro, idly stroking the long flowing white moustache and playing with the curling ends as they grew from his face. "I do hope you will find my lesson most enlightening and rewarding," he added before jumping down and leaping onto his own desk. "For the benefit of Mr. Atwell here, geography and environmental studies are different in what way?" he asked, looking around at his pupils.

"Sir! Sir!" called Cooper who sat directly behind Dominic with his hand raised high in the air.

"Yes, Cooper," acknowledged Mr. Osorro.

"Environmental studies examines the effects of nature and our actions while geography is a direct study of the different places we live."

"Very good," said Mr. Osorro. "And just where did we get to last lesson...anyone but Cooper please." He looked about the class until his eyes rested on the three figures at the back of the class. "Yes, Blue," he stated, "you seem to have a lot to say."

All eyes shifted to the back of the class toward the mandrill who looked to the floor. "No sir," he snarled.

"No sir, what?" asked Mr. Osorro. "You seem to be very vocal with your... how shall I say...friends." Blue shrugged. "Michigan!" snapped the small emperor tamarin, "What about you? No... Dakota?" Both gorillas shook their heads in turn. "See me after class all three of you! I will not tolerate talking unless I specifically request your interaction," he snapped. "Last lesson we looked at areas of Central Africa and the clearance of much of the forest habitat and conservation in the area." He turned his back on the

138

class and pulled a diagram from his desk and placed it neatly over the board. "This is an area known to the humans as Gibraltar," he said. "It is a small landmass between mainland Europe and Africa and where our species and humans co-habit. It is one of a few areas where both cultures co-exist, and you could define both species. Can anyone else tell me any other places where humans and apes live together?"

"Zoos," whispered Blue at the back of the class. The remark was met with complete silence from the class and Blue frowned at the lack of laughter. He glanced testily toward the two gorillas at either side of him, who both sat with their heads down.

"I will not tolerate any further disruption in my classroom, Blue!" snapped Mr. Osorro. "One more remark like that and you sir shall be on report. Do I make myself clear?" The mandrill nodded and snarled as he stared at Dominic, who smiled at the primate's discomfort. It's started, he thought and waved his hand in the air. "Yes Dominic?" asked Mr. Osorro.

"India," he stated.

"Quite right my boy," clapped the tamarin. "Now if you turn your books to page forty-seven you will see examples of how man and ape can live in harmony together."

Dominic felt a gush of smugness wash over him as the images on the pages of the book stared back at him. Monkeys running over rooftops and sitting with people on rocks and buildings. He hazarded a quick glance toward the back of the class and the glowering mandrill who sat stock still, quietly seething with his book firmly closed. It had begun…

Chapter Twenty-Three
GOING BANANAS

"Who do you think you are?" demanded a gruff voice from behind the bench. Dominic ignored the question and instead watched as Fiver laughed with Brannigan. "Well?" demanded the voice again, slightly louder than before and gaining the attention of several primates on the surrounding tables. Again, Dominic chose to ignore the remark and feigned a false laugh at some unspoken joke. He could feel the tension begin as eyes from the other tables watched intently and a tidal wave of whispers swept over the courtyard. "I'm talking to you!" snapped the voice, and still Dominic chose to ignore the speaker and leant forward and whispered something into Fiver's ear, to which the small ape threw his head back and laughed loud, slapping a hand against his leg. He could feel the anger growing in the monkey behind him and smirked to himself. "Human," growled the voice, and this time Dominic felt a thick heavy hand push his back. He realised from the strength in the push and the size of the hand, this was not the mandrill, but one of his two gorilla henchmen.

Dominic turned as though this was the first time he had seen the mandrill and feigned surprise, "Oh! Hello Blue, I didn't see you there," he lied, smiling while casting a glance from the mandrill to each of the gorillas at his side. "Been here long?" he asked sweetly.

"Don't give me that!" snapped Blue. "You know damn well that I was talking to you!" His words were growing in volume and attracting more attention. This was exactly what Dominic was hoping for, cause enough disruption and gain attention, then…

"I'm sorry," he apologized, "but I think you are mistaken." He spoke carefully, choosing his words deliberately and with enough volume so others within earshot would hear. "I was just sitting here having a laugh with my friends," he waved at the others at the table, who shifted uncomfortably under the scrutiny of the mandrill. "I really didn't know you were there."

"Don't you give me that!" demanded Blue, repeating his words.

"Really," smiled Dominic. "You've already said that you must be losing your memory." He laughed at the mandrill and could see a cloud of anger mask the face of the monkey. "Can I help you with something?" he asked, remaining calm.

Blue clenched his fist and leant forward close to the boy's face. Dominic could feel the warmth of his breath as it touched his face and smelt the sickly tang of rotting fruit on his breath. "Watch your back boy," snarled Blue, baring his teeth and running his tongue over a long gleaming fang.

"Whoah!" commented Dominic, pulling away and waving a hand in his face. "What have you been eating!" he exclaimed laughing. "Smells like something's died in there!" his remark gained a few subdued laughs and giggles from some of the primates surrounding the area. Blue cast a look around him and was met by a sea of faces, some were puzzled at the sudden shift in power between man and ape, others were smiling; amused by the torrent of abuse their own abuser was now receiving.

"Don't push me," warned Blue, forcing his hand roughly into Dominic's shoulder. "Remember what I did to you in the Jungle," he said softly.

Dominic winched slightly under the pressure on his shoulder, and the words which hid no lies but were laden with malice stung and ate at his soul. "You did nothing to me Blue," he lied loudly enough so others could hear his words. "I fell...and as far as I can remember you were busy hiding in the corner of the gym out of the way." He laughed and slowly stood from the bench and stepped closer to Blue, looking directly into the monkey's eyes. "I'm not scared of you," he said loudly and took another step closer to Blue. Their bodies were almost pressed against each other's, their faces close to each other.

"You should be," snarled Blue.

"You don't scare me!" shouted Dominic louder, gaining further attention from the other tables. Most of the children in the courtyard now sat watching the events unfold between Blue and Dominic.

"Boss…" said Dakota cautiously.

"Shut up!" snapped Blue, standing his ground before Dominic. "I'm warning you."

"Or what!" snapped Dominic leaning forward and whispering in the mandrill's ear. "You push me out of a tree again? You hit me? Do your best! Every time you hit me, I'll get up again and stand before you. Every time you shout at me, I'll shout back. You're a bully Blue, and I am not afraid of you."

"Boss…" said Michigan this time, looking around at the growing crowd.

"You should be afraid of me!" snapped Blue.

"Boss," repeated Dakota.

"You should be very afraid," he smiled at the boy as he enforced his words with a rough hand against his shoulder. But instead of backing away, Dominic took another step closer to the mandrill and shook his head at the monkey.

"Boss," whispered Michigan.

"What is it!" snapped Blue still meeting Dominic's stare.

"Look." Blue slowly turned his head from Dominic at the gorilla's request and gazed about the courtyard. The sight that met him made him step backwards involuntarily. The small crowd of primates who had taken an interest in the argument had grown, and now most of the children in the courtyard were gathered around the pair in a tight circle. Blue looked at the tide of faces and could see fear replaced by determination and recognised many faces that he had victimized all turning to anger and defiance. He turned back to look at Dominic, and his attention was caught by the apes behind him. Slowly Fiver stood from his seat and stood behind Dominic with his hands clenched and glared angrily at Blue. Brannigan followed suit, followed by Penny and Cooper. Blue backed away slowly, flanked by his two gorillas, and watched the group as they moved slowly across the courtyard. The group of primates watched as the trio sulked away.

"We did it!" laughed Fiver, clapping his hands and jumping before Dominic.

"No," said Dominic, quietly looking past his friend at the disappearing figure. "It's not over yet."

Chapter Twenty-Four

MONKEY BUSINESS

D ominic sat alone in his room and rubbed his hands together.
His thoughts strayed back to the incident in the courtyard,
and he sighed heavily. It had started he thought, now he had to
plan his next move carefully and act before Blue could. He knew
that the mandrill would be angry and he had to move swiftly before
retribution could enforce Blue's reputation as Alpha. He swung his
legs onto the bed and folded his hands behind his head and closed
his eyes, running over various scenarios in his mind...all of which
didn't end well. Images flashed in his head, teeth bared and coated
with saliva, sharply pointed talons, fur, eyes; red and burning with
hatred and his own fear. He admitted to himself as he lay on his
bed with his eyes closed, looking blindly at the ceiling, that he had
felt fear...cold hard fear... like he had never felt before. His legs
had shaken, and his arms quaked, but his voice had remained determined, and that was the important thing when standing up to
a bully, don't show the fear. He had looked into the eyes of Blue
and saw his own reflection staring back in the cold black depths of
those of the mandrill. He let out a long breath and allowed the air
from his lungs to wisp up through the air of his room. A sharp rap
at his door alerted him back into the real world, and he opened his

eyes, straining to the blurred images of his room. A second knock broke the silence and Dominic frowned at the urgency, then swinging his legs from the bed he crossed quickly to the door and pulled at the wooden barrier.

"Hiitsonlyme!" exclaimed Fiver as he bounded across the threshold and onto the bed.

"Fiver…"

"ThatwasamazingtodayimeannotbouncingonyoubedwhatyoudidtoBlue!"

"Fiver!" snapped Dominic. "Slow down."

"Sorry," apologized Fiver. "But I can't help myself," he admitted, grinning from ear to ear as he bounced on the soft mattress beneath his feet.

"I know you're excited, but we've a lot more to do."

"Nonononono," chattered Fiver. "You don't understand, everyone is talking about how you stood up to Blue." He jumped off the bed and grasped Dominic's hands, spinning around the boy. "Children are talking!"

"Fiver, calm down," reinforced Dominic.

"You still don't see, do you?" commented Fiver, releasing his grip on Dominic's hands and sending him spinning onto the bed as he leapt to the door. He pulled at the door and stared out into the corridor, waving as his head disappeared beyond the room. He turned and looked at Dominic, who was still sprawled across his bed and grinned widely revealing an empty passage. Dominic shook his head as he stared past his friend.

"Fiver…"

The small ape held up a finger in the air. "Wait," he whispered. Brannigan moved into view and stepped into the room, gazing around at the décor as he moved toward the window. He was followed by Cooper and Penny, then another smaller chimpanzee, then an orangutan, then lemur, then an aye-aye. One by one pri-

146

mate after primate filed into Dominic's room, all squeezing into the confined space. Dominic looked at the faces, tamarin stood with gibbons, marmoset, and macaque, tarsier and howlers stood side by side. Dominic looked at Fiver as he stood on his bed surrounded by a sea of eager eyes and his friend smiled. "They're here for you," he said.

"I don't understand," commented Dominic, overwhelmed by the sudden interest.

"You stood up to Blue," urged Fiver, glancing across the multitude of primates all gathered in Dominic's room. "At some time, they have all felt the effect of Blue or know someone who has." He leapt onto the bed and flung a hairy arm around his friend. "They've had enough. They all saw how you stood up to Blue and well…" he waved around the room smiling.

"It's not as simple as that."

"They don't care," urged Fiver. "You said yourself he has to be stood up to. Otherwise, he'll continue to bully us."

Dominic nodded, Fiver was right, and he knew from his own experience that as a bully he would continue until someone bigger turned up, or someone stood up to him. He looked at the expectancy in the room and sighed. "This won't be easy," he said eventually to the crowd. "Blue is big and powerful, but he is only one monkey." A chatter rose over the room, and Dominic waved down the sudden commotion, hazarding a glance toward the door. "I know, I know, but you must be silent," he urged.

"What about Michigan and Dakota?" called a small voice from the rear of the room.

"Yeah, what about the gorillas?"

"Please, one problem at a time," reaffirmed Dominic. "The gorillas aren't our main problem. Blue is. Sure, they follow him around like puppies, and they are at his side all the time, but I believe we stand up to Blue, and they will back down."

"How can you be sure?" asked Cooper.

"That's just it, I can't, but what I do know is that they are not as strong as all of us together." He could see Fiver edging through the crowd as he spoke, his eyes glancing from face to face, then back at Dominic and smiling. He frowned as he wondered what his friend was doing, but continued addressing his audience. "One on one, Blue is stronger and faster than most of us, but together he is not stronger than all of us."

Fiver came to a stop close to a small group of female baboons, and Dominic sighed inwardly as Fiver grinned at Kiki J, who folded her arms, stuck her nose in the air and turned her back on the small chimp. "If we stand together..." he continued as he caught a glance at Penny, who was watching Fiver with her own arms folded across her chest, and her eyes narrowing. "Erm...yeah, if we stand together, then Blue cannot stand against us all." He looked around at the gathering and felt a swelling of confidence wash over him. All those eyes, all those faces, all looking at him, hanging on every word. He glanced over at Fiver and could see he was still making moves toward Kiki J and smiling and shook his head. "Fiver!" he called, distracting his friend. "Pass me a timetable," he held out a hand to the crowd.

"Gotta go," whispered Fiver to Kiki J as he patted down the front of his small red jacket, then moved through the crowd to the bed. He leapt onto the bed and bounced under his own weight for a moment and grinned at his friend. He pulled out the small pamphlet from the inside lining of his jacket and handed the paper to Dominic, who unfolded the leaflet and scanned the lessons.

"Perfect," he muttered to himself, his face breaking into a wide grin. He looked back into the crowd. "What I need you all to do first is spread the word. Tell friends, associates, anybody who will listen, anybody who has suffered at the hands of Blue." He waved the timetable in his hands, getting caught up in the moment and excitement of the situation. "It is important Blue has no idea of what we're planning."

"What are we planning?" asked Fiver.

"This…" Dominic smiled and held the timetable before Fiver pointing at one lesson in particular. The small ape looked back at him confused and shrugged his shoulders. "Right, this is important. This is what we are going to do…"

A sudden loud knock broke the moment and caused many of the occupants to jump in surprise. Dominic and Fiver looked at each other confused for a moment. "You expecting anybody?" asked Fiver.

"I wasn't expecting you," Dominic admitted and climbed off the bed and into the throng of primates. Forcing his way through the different types of ape and monkey he marvelled at all these different species all here gathered together as one. The knocking at the door came again and echoed through the room, the sound bouncing off the walls and invading Dominic's senses. "All right," he complained as he reached for the handle. He paused with his hand over the handle for a moment and turned to the apes around him and waved his hands down as though pressing down against a heavy weight and signalling for the children to calm down and hush. He wrapped his fingers around the handle and pulled open the door to reveal the form of…

Dakota.

Chapter Twenty-Five

A MISTRUST OF TRUST

The large gorilla stood framed in the door and strained its big strong neck over the head of Dominic and gazed into the room at the huddle of frightened faces. "I alone," he grunted, his low-pitched tones were unsteady, and his grasp of the language was gutted and poor. "I speak," he said pushing past the boy and forcing his way into the room. Dominic watched him as he pushed his way through the crowd and sat in the corner of the room and stared blankly at the floor.

A chatter erupted from the occupants of the room, and they began to push and surge toward the door, which Dominic closed firmly, locking the outside world…well…outside. "Quiet!" he shouted over the growing noise and picked his way through the worried children. He stopped just short of the clearance that had enveloped around Dakota as he took his place alone in the corner. He looked down at the gorilla who scratched an unseen itch on the back of his neck…his thick neck… with his large stubby fingers. Despite his size and the raw power that the gorilla gave off, Dominic could see a hint of sadness in those eyes. He felt a hand on his arm, and Fiver caught his attention, panic fleeting across his face and Dominic placed a reassuring hand on his friend's and nodded. Then, reaching for a banana in the fruit bowl on the desk nearby, he sat on the floor in front of the behemoth and held out the small yellow fruit in his outstretched hand. "For you," he said uncertainly, hoping he sounded strong but still hearing a waver in his own voice.

"Dakota like," grunted the large gorilla as he took the fruit gingerly from Dominic. The banana was dwarfed by his mighty black palm, and Dominic watched as he raised the yellow skin to his mouth and delicately peeled back to reveal the ripe flesh within. Even at this distance he could feel an air of intimidation at the sheer size of the gorilla and marvelled at the grace with which he took a bite into the fruit, his gleaming white teeth slicing through the flesh of the banana and staining his black fur around his face.

"Dakota…" said Dominic softly, his eyes not leaving the figure sitting before him. "What are you doing here?"

"Blue," said the gorilla simply as he took a second bite. A chatter of voices erupted around them as Dominic watched as small chunks of banana fell from his mouth as he spoke.

"Oh my!" squealed Cooper. "He knows!" The small golden tamarin leapt from Brannigan's back where he had perched for most of the meeting. "We're doomed!"

"Cooper!" snapped Dominic, turning his head slightly and shooting Cooper a silencing glance. "Explain," he said softly to Dakota.

The gorilla swept the final piece of banana into his mouth and sat with the empty skin in his hand and glanced around waving the fruit in his hand…his large mighty hands. "He not know me here," he grunted in his broken English.

"Then why are you here?"

"He mean to Dakota," confided the gorilla in a hushed tone.

"But you're…I mean look at you!" squealed Fiver.

"It has to be a trick!" exclaimed Cooper, hiding behind the

larger chimp.

"No…no!" exclaimed Dakota, raising a large hand and bringing a flood of panic through the room. The great ape fell silent as chaos erupted around him in the room and he shuffled his large frame round to face the wall, tracing his thick fingers across the smooth paintwork as he fell silent in thought.

"Please!" shouted Dominic, raising his hands in the air at the clambering chatter of frightened children. Then he turned back to Dakota and placed his hands on his crossed legs and looked at the gorilla. "Go on," he urged.

"Dakota want to learn," his soft words belied his strength as he shuffled back to face the group. "But Blue make fun of Dakota." He pressed his fingers into his heaving chest. "Dakota's parents send him and brother to school to learn. To be better. We come, and Blue make fun. He strong and mean. Everybody fear Blue. He Alpha, we follow Alpha."

"But you're stronger than he is," exclaimed Dominic.

"He Alpha," Dakota was struggling to find the correct words as he spoke and his frustration could be seen in his eyes. "All scared of Blue when we come. He strong. We learn at home to listen to the silverback, our Alpha. The way it is."

"Then it's wrong," moaned Dominic.

"The way it is," Dakota said, nodding and looked at Dominic. "Then you come," he reached out his arm and jabbed the boy in the chest with his curled knuckle. "You know not he Alpha. You stand up to Blue. You strong. You Alpha."

"No, I'm not," admitted Dominic. "I'm just a boy."

"No," said Dakota slowly. "You strong."

"No," said Dominic again. "I'm not, but we strong…sorry, we are strong." He raised his hand from his lap and moved it behind him at the gathered children. "Together we can show Blue that we don't have to be pushed around."

"Dakota like that," grunted the great ape. "Dakota just want to learn."

"What about your brother?" called Cooper from the crowd.

"Michigan," said Dakota quietly. "He not know I here," he admitted eventually. "He no like Dakota, he not want to learn. He think it waste of time. He want to be alpha like Blue."

"If we could stop Blue, would you be willing to stand against your own brother?" asked Dominic.

Dakota nodded sagely and stared down at the floor, "Dakota just want to learn."

"That's settled then, we go ahead as agreed."

"No, no, no" exclaimed Cooper. "That's not settled, there is nothing good about this!" he squealed in a high-pitched voice. "How can we expect to trust him of all people?" he pointed a finger toward Dakota. "He's been in the middle of our persecution for months, and now we're asked to simply trust him! I think not."

"Why not? He's just in as much danger as all of us!" stated Dominic.

"Because he's…he's…Dakota!"

"How can I trust you?" accused Dominic at Cooper. "Or you?" he said pointing to Fiver. "Or you?" pointing at a small aye-aye. "Or you?" his finger spun toward a red howler. "Or any of you?" The room fell in silence as Dominic continued. "As I see it, anyone in this room could lose their bottle and squeal to Blue in favour of protection or favouritism. Dakota is just like the rest of us, and while he hasn't suffered at the hands of Blue, he has suffered mentally." Dominic stood with new-found confidence behind the gorilla and placed a hand on his shoulder. "He's as much of a victim as we are."

"If Dominic trusts him, then so do I," said Fiver smiling through the crowd at Dominic, before sending off a small wave in the direction of Kiki J, who rolled her eyes at the advances of the chimp.

"I'm not sure," murmured Cooper.

"All it would take is any one of us to panic when we see Blue and tell him our plan," said Dominic gently. "One word…" he let his words sink into the crowd and could see the faces of his audience's glance toward their neighbour. "We have to trust because it's all we have. If we lose our trust, then we lose our soul."

"What we do?" asked Dakota, "Blue strong."

"We'll have to do it quickly before anyone becomes too scared," remarked Dominic, pulling the timetable from his pocket and glancing over the words on the paper. He nodded as he read, "Third period tomorrow…Mr. Bonobo's class." A small wave of chatter exploded across the room at the news. "It's perfect," breathed Dominic, looking about him. "Now, this is what we'll do…"

Chapter Twenty-Six

A PENNY FOR FIVER

The morning had passed relatively quietly as Dominic sat and reflected on the last few hours and the events to come. The sun basked down on his skin and warmed him as he watched the small groups scattered about the courtyard. He remembered the plan he had made last night. He knew that they would have to act quickly and he would need the perfect opportunity…and there it was…period three. The plan had come to him pretty quickly, once the lesson had been decided upon, now everything depended on secrecy. He cast a glance around the courtyard and could feel the tension amongst some of the other groups. Dakota sat stock still and unmoving with his brother and Blue. Dominic felt a slight worry grumble in the pit of his stomach. Did he trust the gorilla, he couldn't be sure. For all he knew Dakota had told Blue everything, and the mandrill was already planning his own form of retribution.

"Whatyoudoing?" chirped Fiver as he bound up to the table and followed Dominic's gaze. "Oh," he said quietly. The mandrill looked across the courtyard at Dominic and caught his attention for a moment and grinned a sickly grin at the boy, revealing a row of razor-sharp teeth. 'Did he know?' Thought Dominic, was he onto them? There was no point in worrying, not yet. His thoughts strayed to the morning lessons and wondered how easily and smoothly they had both gone. Both Food Technology with Mrs. Nasalis and Social Studies with Miss Gibson had gone quite quietly. He remembered how the small proboscis monkey had shown the class various food groups and berries found within the Amazon basin and the techniques that the indigenous groups used to harvest the fruit, as well as berries to avoid and the dangers of collecting rotting substances. Then, of course, Miss Gibson had taught them the effects of social grooming within large groups and the benefits of living in larger groups. The gibbon kept Dominic and Blue at opposite ends of the class, but Dominic had noted that the teacher still kept a wary eye on both pupils.

"Just thinking," murmured Dominic, eventually answering Fiver's question. "Do you think he knows?" queried Dominic. "He keeps looking over."

"What do you expect Dom?" stated Fiver. "When you can't keep your eyes off him, either that or he thinks you fancy him!" The small chimp laughed at his joke and Dominic responded with a nervous smile.

"I suppose," sighed Dominic. "It's just…we only have one shot at this and if it doesn't work."

"Dom, you have most of school behind us and all of our year," he laughed and nudged Dominic's arm. "What could go wrong?"

"Him for a start," Dominic commented, as Michigan spoke to Dakota and the large gorilla stared down at the floor as his brother rose and spoke down to him. "What if he cracks?" He watched as Michigan nudged his brother, then flicked his cap onto the floor and roared with laughter. Blue nodded and pushed Dakota's books on the floor and kicked them absently across the dirt, laughing as Dakota sat staring down at the crumpled pages.

"By the looks of things, we won't have anything to worry about.

Now…if you excuse me," he leapt from the table and straightened to full height, breathing in deeply and puffing his chest out. "I have a certain lady that needs my attention." He laughed and pointed toward the baboon in the pink dress who was sitting with her friends.

"Fiver!" snapped Dominic. "Wait."

The small ape deflated and looked at his friend concerned. "What is it? You nervous?"

"No, it's just…"

"Come on," urged Fiver. "I need to look like a hero before I make my move," he eased a hand through his hair and laughed.

"Before we go to the class, I need to do one final thing."

"Like?"

"I need to sort this…" he leant forward, his smile fading as he whispered to his friend. "Sorry."

"Why what for?" he flicked a quick glance toward Kiki J, then back at Dominic. "Can't this wait?" he said urgently.

"No, not this," he patted the seat by his and urged his friend to take a seat. Fiver sat and looked at Dominic, unsure what he was going to say. "Look, Kiki J…" Dominic said uncertainly.

"I know, isn't she amazing?" cooed Fiver. "Her silky brown hair, her long regal black snout, those deep penetrating brown eyes and those buttocks! Wow, those big round pink buttocks. I may be allergic to bananas, but I'd share one with her any day!" He smiled as he spoke and gripped his knees, rocking slightly in his seat.

"Kiki J," repeated Dominic.

"Is amazing."

"Isn't interested," sighed Dominic.

"What?"

"She isn't interested, Five. Look at her." He followed Fiver's gaze at the group of baboons as they laughed and looked at another group of male baboons.

"No, she's just playing hard to get."

"Hard!" exclaimed Dominic. "I've seen rocks softer than her! I'd say she is impossible for you." He felt sorry for his friend, but he couldn't let him do this. "Fiver," he said softly, "I don't want to see you hurt or make a fool of yourself. Kiki J is nice…for a baboon, but that's it. She's a baboon, and she's into other baboons. Not gorillas, not gibbons and certainly not chimpanzees. I'm sorry, but she's just not into you," he said, and Fiver cast his head down.

"Why?" bemoaned Fiver. "Why you telling me?"

"Because there is someone who likes you," the small ape looked up, and Dominic could see tears forming in his eyes. "Someone close to you," he smiled as he spoke.

"Look," snapped Fiver, "I'm flattered and everything, I really am, but…"

"Not me!" snapped Dominic grinning. "Idiot!" he placed his hand gently under Fiver's chin and swivelled his head around to face another smaller chimp…

"Penny," whispered Fiver astoundingly.

"Yes, Penny," agreed Dominic.

"But…she's a friend," complained Fiver.

"I know," agreed Dominic again.

"My best friend."

"Your best friend," whispered Dominic.

"You know what I mean, my oldest friend."

"She likes you."

"I know she does."

"She cares for you," whispered Dominic quietly as Fiver stared at Penny.

"I care for her," admitted Fiver.

"She worries about you."

"She does?"

"She does" confirmed Dominic. "Do yourself a favour, Fiver. Would you settle for someone who is just there, someone you like, but ultimately doesn't love you or somebody who really cares? Somebody who thinks about you every day. Somebody who cares and worries about you. Somebody who only thinks of you twice a day."

"Twice a day," murmured Fiver, looking at Penny as though he had just seen her for the first time.

"Morning and night."

"Morning and night," repeated Fiver. He turned suddenly and looked at Dominic, his mouth turning into a large grin. "She's my best friend. She IS my best friend," he said softly. "I never realised before, but I would do anything for her," he said.

"That's why you should talk to her, tell her," said Dominic gently. Fiver stood up and looked down at the sitting boy. "I'll wait here," Dominic said. "Then back to business."

Fiver nodded and turned away from the bench and bounding across the courtyard he called as he bounced, "Penny!" he called as he ran over the uneven ground. "Penny!"

Chapter Twenty-Seven

WHO FLUNG THE DUNG?

D ominic stood as he watched his friend as he spoke to Penny.
He could see a smile spread across her face and through
her red lipstick lined mouth, her teeth shone out through her fur
encrusted face. She threw her arms around the small chimp, and
she pulled him close to her body, the two joining as one as Fiver
returned her affections by wrapping his black-furred arms around
her body. He felt slightly uncomfortable as the two chimps stared
into each other's eyes. Dominic turned away before they kissed.

He turned his attention toward the school and more specifically the block which stood in the distance, rising through the tree
encrusted crescent like a waking dragon stirring from an ancient
slumber. The Madagascar block stood back from the rest of the
school and was only accessible via a thin winding pathway which
led from the recreation area which he stood in now and past the
Amazon block which he had recognised from the Communication
class with Mr. Reddington and the Sumatra block which stood in
the centre of the school site. He hadn't spent as much time in this
block as he knew he should have and realised how much time he
had actually missed. A thought struck him that he had never had
before, can I make up the time that I have missed, he thought to

himself as he attempted to blend in with the crowd, picking his way across the gravel-lined pathway, past the watering hole, looking out over the vast playing fields. At every school he had attended, he had never been particularly bothered if he had done well, but something here made him feel as though he needed to succeed.

He didn't know if he had to prove himself to his fellow pupils, or himself. He was, after all, the only human in the school and was probably seen by most as a threat. He felt he had something to prove not just for himself, but also the good that man could provide. Then there was this niggling doubt in his mind that if he failed here, then he would remain a failure for the rest of his life. He knew this was his last chance, and he had to do well just to prove to himself that he could do it. The building reared up before him as he neared to the block and the smell of the interior hit him like a wall, reminding him of what lay ahead. Because of the nature of the lesson, Dominic did not have to attend this particular class, but Dominic also knew if his plan was to succeed, then this would be the ideal location.

His throat gagged as he approached the building and he could feel his stomach churn as the pungent smell repelled his nostrils. He looked about as the other children walked, ran and swung toward the building, laughing and smiling. They were used to the smell he supposed, and forced his legs along the path, listening to his feet as they crunched into the path. He could see Blue ahead of him, flanked by the two gorillas as they stalked up the path laughing as the mandrill mocked a small baboon's walk before pushing it into an overgrown bush. Dakota glanced back down the path and nodded toward Dominic as he paused with his brother and pointed at the baboon as it sprawled in the bushes.

"What's the matter?" he heard Blue laugh. "Don't you know how to walk?" he laughed and bounded away up the path, with the gorillas walking slowly behind, Michigan nudging his brother and winking.

Dominic stopped by the baboon and held out a hand for the ape. "It won't be long," he whispered as he hauled him out of the bush.

"Will it work though?" asked the ape, looking at the back of the mandrill as he disappeared through the gaping maw of the school building.

Dominic nodded. "As long as we all stick together, the plan will work," he said, hoping his voice sounded confident. He stopped before the building and stood looking up at the towering structure. He could see the windows scattered across the front of the two-story block, and up the outside of the building tendrils of ivy ran along the pebble-dashed brickwork.

Fiver slapped him on the back and leant over his shoulder. "Thisisit," he laughed and stared through the open door. "Coming?"

Fiver was right, this was it. Part of him knew they had to stand up to Blue, while part of him wanted to run and hide. The doors opened inwardly, and Dominic stared down the long corridor into the darkness that stretched before him. He entered the building and walked slowly along the corridor, passing several small rooms, considering each room as he passed. He could see several tables and chairs lining each class and various posters displaying pictures of monkeys on the wall with images of food and waste from each animal. At the end of the corridor stood a pair of large wooden framed glass doors, with heavy green curtains covering the opening. Dominic pushed his way through the material and stood in a large open room. The smell was intense, and Dominic recoiled, his hand covering his nose as he stood on the threshold of the hall.

"What's up?" mocked Blue as he rose up close to Dominic. "You too sensitive to be here?" he laughed as he approached threatening the boy with his presence.

"The only offensive thing here is you," retorted Dominic, forcing his hand to his side. "My word!" he said loudly sniffing in the air. "What's that strange smell?" he called, then looked toward the mandrill. "Oh, I know!" he exclaimed. "It's you!"

Blue snarled at Dominic and lunged forward, only being stopped by a thick paw placed on his arm. Blue paused, his anger rising through his body and looked at his arm, tracing it back to the body of Dakota who was standing with his hand on his arm. "Dakota!" he snapped. The gorilla never said a word, simply nodded toward the door where an elderly figure had pushed his way through the curtains. Blue nodded and whispered savagely toward Dominic. "You're lucky this time boy!" he spat quietly.

"I've told you before Blue, I'm not scared of you," said Dominic softly, taking a step toward Blue.

"You should be," whispered the mandrill, leaning his face close to Dominic's and allowing his hot breath to stain Dominic's face.

"Look around you," smiled Dominic. Blue took a step back and cast his gaze around the hall at the pupils gathering around the walls. Faces of all shapes and sizes were staring at the two as they faced each other. "They can see, I'm not scared of you," he said carefully. "You've no power over me."

"That will change," snarled Blue, his fist clenched. "But not here," he glanced toward the old chimp who had taken his place at the front of the hall and was now looking out over the pupils.

The ape was dressed in a small tweed jacket and plain black trousers and wore small half mooned glasses perched at the end of his nose. His once black fur was tinged by grey and ran across his face and sprouted from the ends of his jacket. "Children," he said carefully and slowly, looking over the top of the glasses and scanning his class.

"Good afternoon Mr. Bonobo," chorused the children.

"Dominic Atwell," wheezed the teacher through cracked lips,

shocked at the inclusion of the boy in the class. "Are you sure you should be here?" he enquired.

"Yes, sir," said Dominic loudly.

"You do understand the nature of this class?"

"Yes sir," confirmed Dominic, pulling a set of plastic gloves from his pocket. He held them up in the air and waved them toward Mr. Bonobo.

"Very well…if you're sure, there are after all no records of your species doing this activity," Mr. Bonobo paused and looked across the class. "Right, I suppose if there are no further objections, we should begin. Michigan…Dakota, if you could," he said toward the two large gorillas. The two pupils walked toward the back of the hall and slid open a set of sliding doors, and between them, they removed three large blue barrels from the storage room. They carried each of the barrels, one at a time into the centre of the floor before returning to their position close to the wall. "In the last lesson, we spoke extensively about the usage of faeces for defensive practices. Today, we will look at the difference between the usage of poo in contrast as an aggressive nature." He walked over to the three barrels and removed one lid after another, revealing a mass of brown, steaming waste. The old chimp drove his hand into the faeces and held it close to his nose. "Ah, fresh," he smiled as he dropped the substance back into the barrel. "Now, if you can make three civil lines and collect yourselves a container of poo. You will find the containers placed at the end of the table, there…" he said pointing, "and return to the edge of the wall while I set up the equipment."

Dominic took his position in line behind Fiver, who was bouncing on the spot acting like an over-excited child on Christmas morning. "Calm down," he whispered leaning forward. Fiver nodded his understanding, and slowly the line moved forward as each primate took a container of poo from the barrel. Dominic stared down into the barrel and felt his stomach wretch, the smell was overwhelming, and his hands hovered over the edge of the barrel.

"Is there a problem, Dominic?" asked Mr. Bonobo.

"No sir," said Dominic, trying not to breathe in the obnoxious fumes. He thrust the container into the soft brown faeces, careful not to stain his gloves and weighed it in his hands before moving into line with the other children.

Mr. Bonobo walked up and down the line, as he surveyed the children in his group, then suddenly turned and placed his hand in the barrel, withdrawing a hand full of faeces. He stood on his hind legs and weighed the poo in his hand. Looking at the class, he lowered himself down onto one hand, his other still holding the brown substance. "As we have already spoken about, this is our most important natural weapon," he said, indicating to his hand where the poo sat moist and glistening in the sunlight from the window. Dominic thought for a moment that the chimp was going to throw it at one of the children as he stood weighing the poo in his hand. "The difference between attack and defence is your stance. With defence, your position is very much on your rear foot, with your body placed toward the side. The elevation of the faeces is therefore only reactionary and therefore can only obtain a certain trajectory. Today, however, as you will see from this position… that you will be able to run at speed on either two or three legs at your victim and launch your faeces at greater speed and elevation." He moved his legs forward in to an aggressive stance as he spoke. He held the poo in his hand and ran across the floor toward large boards which had been placed at the end of the room. As he ran across the floor, he pulled his arm from beneath his body and raised it above his body, launching the faeces against the boards.

Dominic watched for a moment and glanced down into the container in his hands…this was it…

He was aware that Mr. Bonobo was talking to the class as he stared into the brown substance. He sighed and pushed his fingers into the container, allowing the warmth of the faeces to caress his hand beneath the latex gloves. It felt soft to the touch and squeezed through Dominic's fingers as he curled his hand into a fist. He heard the squelch of wet waste material as it ran through his fingers and smeared his hand. The smell invaded his nostrils, and Dominic silently prayed that the latex didn't rip as he moved his hand slowly through the container. He was aware that several eyes were moving nervously toward him, as though waiting for a signal. He sighed and moved his hand, covered in brown, dripping dung out of the container. He watched as small globules fell to the floor and splashed against the cold solid wood. Dominic pulled his hand back…

Blue was standing between Dakota and Michigan holding his container. He was smiling, as the thought of slipping and covering that boy had crossed his mind…that would teach him, same as it had in the gym. A flash caught his eye as something flew into eyeline, and the sound of his name caused him to turn his head slightly as something wet hit the side of his head…

Chapter Twenty-Eight
WHAT'S BROWN AND SMELLS
OF BANANA?

Time stood still.

Blue felt something warm stain his fur and stood in shock. He looked down at his fur and traced the slow descent of the soft brown substance as it flowed over his thick fur. He could still feel the sting against his cheek from the impact and the smell which crept and caressed his nose stung his senses. He looked across the hall, and his eyes met those of Dominic, and he felt the hostility rise and anger sweep over his body. The boy was standing directly opposite, facing the mandrill with one hand dripping with the waste matter, and the half-empty container in the other.

Dominic scooped a second handful of poo in his hand and dropped the container to the floor. Blue watched in slow motion as his hand pulled back behind his body and snapped forward, launching the faeces in his hand toward him. He turned his head as the substance struck him fiercely on the chest and matted in his thick fur. Mr. Bonobo turned and watched the end event and held his hands in the air shouting, "No!" Blue stood, his chest heaving as his anger threatened to consume his body. He could feel his face turning a deep crimson as the blood flushed through his body. His fists clenched and he dropped his container, abandoning any thoughts of dirty retribution, he looked at Dominic with pure hatred boiling over. "Oh my!" exclaimed the old chimp, and he quickly vacated the hall. "Miss Hawthorne! Miss Hawthorne!" he called as he ran from the hall.

Blue glanced sideways towards the gorillas and clicking his stubby fingers, he pointed toward Dominic. Michigan nodded and roared moving forward across the wooden floor. The sound of his scream echoed through the room and bounced off the walls as he approached Dominic on his hind legs, his fists raised high above his head. By Dominic, there was a blur of activity, and the boy felt a rush of air as something large and black moved quickly past him. Michigan moved fast through the room, close to the boy…then something large slammed into his shoulder, taking him off his feet and he landed in a heap on the floor. Michigan growled from the ground and rubbed his hurt shoulder, then pulled himself to a sitting position and stared up at his attacker. Dakota…his brother, stood over him, standing tall on his back legs staring down at the prone form of his brother. He lowered himself onto all four legs and leant close to Michigan's head and snorted warm air into his face.

"Dakota," whispered the prone ape. Dakota frowned and held up a single finger between his brother's eyes and waved it back and forth.

"It's over brother," he growled, then turned to Blue, looking at the shocked animal. He prowled across the floor of the hall and stood behind Dominic, raising himself to his full height and crossing his arms behind the boy.

"What is this!" demanded Blue as he watched a sudden shift in power.

"The end, Blue," said Dominic smiling. "It's over!"

"I'll still rip you to pieces!" snarled the mandrill.

"And then what Blue?" called Dominic. "First me, then Dakota, then Fiver, then who…" he waved about the ever-increasing circle of primates crowding around them. "If I fall, there will be someone waiting to take my place, then someone else…and someone else. It'll never end Blue. Your time is over. Back down," he warned.

"Never!" snapped Blue, clenching his fists and running forward toward Dominic.

"So be it," sighed the boy. "Now!" he shouted.

The circle of children around the pair unleashed a symphony of poo upon the mandrill. Cheers and laughter erupted uncontrollably as the children lost control. Years and months of pent-up fear and anger finally flowed out of each child who had suffered at the hands of Blue and his friends. Hands and arms moved swiftly as each child grasped at their container and pulled vast handfuls of faeces from the small boxes and threw the waste at the monkey. Piece after piece struck Blue and slowly he fell under the weight of the attack and lay on the floor, his arms desperately trying to protect his head from the hailstorm of brown missiles. Dakota stood tall and nodded toward his brother, who stood meekly and joined him next to one of the large blue barrels. He indicated at the barrel and bent to lift the base of the container, Michigan copying his every move, reluctantly at first, then slowly the second ape began smiling as they walked across the floor to the cowering Blue. The crowd separated as the two gorillas moved through the children and stood over Blue, holding the barrel over the monkey's head. The sound of laughter grew as some of the smaller primates leapt and somersaulted, beating their chests as the noise became unbearable. Blue looked up briefly as a shadow descended over him, "poo" he whispered as the two gorillas poured the contents over him.

"What is the meaning of this?" came a voice from the door. All faces turned to look at the figure of Miss Hawthorne as she stood framed in the sunlight, cast from the main door and travelling down the corridor. "Dominic Atwell!"

Chapter Twenty-Nine

KING DOM

"I do not condone any of this behaviour!" stormed Miss Hawthorne as she stood behind her desk, her hands pressed hard against the wooden surface. She wore a frown on her face, and her eyes pinned Dominic in the seat opposite her. "What you have done is absolutely deplorable at best!" Behind her Dominic could see Mr. Hindle framed in the sunlight, his arms crossed in defiant support of the headmistress. "That poor child, to be covered in... in...waste!" she raged for want of a better word. "That behaviour is disgusting!" Mr. Hindle nodded vigorously behind her, but Dominic was sure he could see the traces of a smile fighting at the edges of his lips. The chair he sat in swamped his body, and he pressed down into the red leather. He was aware of Grant standing next to the chair, and his gaze followed the powerful arms up his body to his passive face. As normal, the giant of a gorilla bore no emotion, just stood there with one hand resting on the back of the chair, while the other fell limply by his large bulk. "To go to class and be treated like that...well, I have no words for it," continued Miss Hawthorne, sighing and turning to Mr. Hindle. "What do you think Eronymous?" she asked.

"I...err...well..." stammered the deputy, still forcing down a smile.

"You see!" snapped Miss Hawthorne, sitting in her chair and leaning forward on her desk. "Even poor Mr. Hindle is lost for words." Dominic was aware of a fourth figure at the back of the room, a figure who hid in the shadows, but could be heard every now and again sniggering under his/her breath. "Dominic, you realise what you have done is completely unacceptable, don't you?" she said softly, looking at the small child in the chair. Dominic nodded mutely and lowered his head, trying not to smile at the thought of Blue covered in poo. "I know that you've not had it easy at Hazeldene with certain individuals, but I cannot be seen to condone any of this behaviour."

"I'm sorry miss," whispered Dominic, talking into the floor.

"It's a start I suppose," she sighed. "For the record, no one else in the class has actually seen anything, so I'm just going on the evidence of Blue's statement…and that of Mr. Bonobo." Miss Hawthorne shuffled a pile of papers and held one sheet before her eyes and read it through her half-moon glasses, "Mr. Bonobo claims that Blue was hit by a handful of excrement thrown by you," she said, looking at the boy and the figure sniggering at the rear of the room. "What have you to say, Dominic?"

"I did throw the poo Miss," confirmed Dominic.

"So, you are admitting the incident?"

Dominic shook his head, "No Miss, it was an accident."

"In what way?"

"As Mr. Bonobo will tell you, it was my first time in the lesson," he said as innocently as he could. "I did throw the poo, but not at Blue. I was trying to hit the targets, but I didn't realise how slippery the poo was and it slid out of my hand."

"You're claiming it was an accident," said Miss Hawthorne frowning. Dominic nodded as he watched Mr. Hindle raise a hand to his mouth and turn to face the window. "I find this very hard to believe."

"Did Mr. Bonobo see me deliberately throw it at Blue?" asked Dominic.

"Well, no," agreed Miss Hawthorne. "But he did say you had thrown it, and you were standing facing him at the time."

"No, no," denied Dominic. "When I realised what had happened, I did turn to apologize to Blue…that was when he ran to me…to shake my hand, when he slipped and fell into the open barrel."

A chorus of laughter erupted from the rear of the room causing Miss Hawthorne to glance angrily at her colleague. "Mr. Trethorne!" she snapped. "This is no laughing matter…" *at least not yet*, she thought to herself as she stared into the shadows. "Now, Dominic. Are you sure these are the events which led up to the unfortunate incident?" Dominic nodded again, and Miss Hawthorne sighed, looking at another sheet of paper. "Well, while I do have difficulty in believing your story, it does match several other statements taken from various children in the class." She read the words on the paper and placed it neatly on the surface of the table. "Due to the nature of the incident, I cannot ignore certain events which led up to the situation. There has been an altercation between yourself and the pupil in question, and while there is no evidence that this act was deliberate, I do have to take that into account. You may have acted under extreme provocation and sought retribution." She paused to consider her words. "Circumstances leading to the incident have been catalogued by various of my colleagues and noted. However, due to the number of potential pupils involved in this incident, I cannot ignore the evidence laid before me."

"Olive, if I may be so bold," said Mr. Trethorne, moving into the light. Miss Hawthorne nodded. "Dominic has actually done nothing wrong, nothing we can prove, and given that the whole class was involved…how do we punish the entire class?"

"Agreed," confirmed Miss Hawthorne. "Mr. Hindle, your counsel."

He turned from the window smiling. "I'm sorry Olive, but I really think this is hilarious!" he laughed loudly, then tried to regain his composure under her angry scrutiny. "I'm sorry, my dear, but it is. Blue with all the..." his words trailed off as they died in his throat. "It is unfair to punish everyone," he said, eventually composing himself. "Or indeed anyone. We don't have enough information to say what actually happened in the class."

"Blue claims it was a deliberate attack," stated Miss Hawthorne.

"A known troublemaker!" exclaimed Mr. Trethorne.

"That is hardly the point," chided Miss Hawthorne.

"We only have his word, Olive," said Mr. Hindle softly. "And if we take the word of one child over the entire class..."

"Understood," said Miss Hawthorne nodding. She sighed and looked at the papers on the desk, then announced, "I have decided that, while I cannot condone your actions, I do commend your perseverance in continuing lessons, and while I do not know what really happened in class, I do know, by your own admission that you threw the first...err shall we say...stone. That said, I will expect to see you and Blue in detention for the next week. There will be no further action against anyone else in the class." She smiled and looked across the table. "You may go," she said. Dominic stood quietly and moved across the room, he paused as he heard his name spoken. "Dominic," said Miss Hawthorne softly. Dominic turned and stood waiting for her words. Mr. Hindle had placed a hand on her shoulder and was watching as Mr. Trethorne pulled at the door handle. She smiled and said, "Well done."

Dominic stepped out of the room and as the door shut firmly behind him, he was sure he could hear laughing from inside. He could imagine both Mr. Hindle and Mr. Trethorne laughing, while

Miss Hawthorne would be sitting at her desk frowning. Despite all of this, Dominic still could not imagine any form of emotion crossing the impassive face of Grant who he thought would still be standing frozen to the spot by the large leather red chair.

"Dominic!" called Fiver as he walked into the recreation area behind the student block. He had thought about returning to his room, but the sun was so bright and the heat pounded on the floor. He turned to see his friend bound from a nearby tree and settle close to him.

"Fiver," said Dominic smiling.

"What happened?" asked the concerned small chimp.

"Slap on the wrist, don't do it again," laughed Dominic. "We did it," he whispered placing his hands on Fiver's shoulders. "We did."

"There is something you should see," said Fiver solemnly.

"What is it?" concern danced over Dominic's face...had all of his efforts been in vain...surely Blue wasn't...his thoughts were interrupted as the chimp took his hand and lead him through the trees and building toward the dining room.

"Just come and see." The dining room was empty, and Dominic looked around unsure how to feel. Had everything he had planned gone wrong? Fiver stood by the large double doors by the main hall, and he turned smiling, then flung the doors open. Dominic stood in the centre of the dining room and stared into the main hall. There before him stood row after row of expectant faces of all shapes and sizes, different species standing as one. Baboon stood with gorilla, tamarin with chimp, simply looking at this small boy. One by one, each of the animals began a slow clap, turning faster and faster into a chorus of applause, then a tidal wave of cheers washed over the hall. Monkeys and apes leapt into the air and laughed, calling a single name as the noise became deafening.

"Dom! Dom! Dom! Dom!" rang the call.

Dominic felt a sense of pride come over him and for the first time in his life...he felt good.

Chapter Thirty

END OF YEAR

Dominic walked out into the sunlight pulling his case behind
him. It bulged in his hand as he looked around as adult primates milled about the school waiting for their children. The rest
of the year had passed quietly, which was probably a good thing.
Blue had disappeared pretty much following the poo events of Mr.
Bonobo's class…and rightly so. The whole class had stood up to
him and shown that the fear he had generated over the year had
gone. Dominic stood for a moment as the children ran past him,
leaping into the arms of the adults. He received a few sideways
glances from some of the parents, but their focus was soon distracted by their approaching children.

He watched as the two gorilla brothers walked slowly on all
fours across the gravel to meet their parents. Dominic marvelled
at the change in dynamics since that day. Dakota was no longer
the meek brother, who hid behind Michigan and followed in his
wake. Now, he strode purposely at the front, confident and proud
while Michigan trailed behind carrying both of their cases. Dakota
gripped the large silverback firmly and spoke to his mother while
his brother hung back at a respectful distance under the curiously
watchful eye of his father. Dominic turned his attention to Blue

as he walked slowly toward his parents. The mandrill glanced over toward Dominic as he greeted his family and nodded sagely at the boy. He stood for a few minutes watching as Cooper and Penny met their parents, and he felt a pang of sadness that his own parents were not involved in this final day celebration.

"Dominic!" called Fiver, waving as he ran. "Come on, come on," he urged the couple trailing behind him. Dominic couldn't help but smile as he watched the two older chimps being towed behind this excitable ape. "Thisismybestfriend!" cried Fiver as he jumped up and down on the spot. "Itoldyouallabouthim."

"I'm going to miss this," laughed Dominic as he placed his arms around his friend.

"What?" said Fiver.

"You, speaking so fast I can't understand you," the two boys laughed and threw their arms around each other. "Thank you," whispered Dominic in Fiver's ear.

"No," said Fiver smiling, and casting a quick glance in Penny's direction. "Thank you," they grinned at each other and stood awkwardly for a moment before Fiver spoke again. "Will I see you again?"

Dominic shrugged, the smile fading from his lips. "I don't know," he admitted. "It depends on my mum and dad."

"I could speak to them," offered Fiver hopefully.

"No way," laughed Dominic. "A talking chimp would probably give them a heart attack!" He held out his hand and grasped Fiver's in his own and shook it. "Till next time," he said sadly.

Fiver looked at his hand and struggled to regain his smile. "Next time," he agreed and turned away and walked slowly to his parents. He paused and looked back toward Dominic. "It was fun, wasn't it?" he asked.

Dominic smiled and nodded. "Yes," he said softly. Fiver grasped his mother's hand and walked away, leaving Dominic alone with his thoughts.

"Dominic," the soft voice of Miss Hawthorne made him turn and face the steps. "Your parents are waiting," she smiled gently at him and waved inside the building. He followed her into the building and along the lonely corridor. As he walked, he felt the stares of the eyes from each portrait as he walked past, each one giving their judgement, each one with their own story to tell. Mr. Hindle was waiting at the door of the office, and he smiled a kindly smile at Dominic before pushing the door open. He looked past the two adults and into the room, half expecting to see Grant standing over his parents, but instead they sat alone in the office, sinking into the plush leather chairs. They turned as they heard the sound of the door open and Mrs. Atwell rose to her feet and held out her arms.

"My baby!" she cried and ran to Dominic, holding him in her arms. She looked down at him and ran her hand through his hair. "Have you been good? Did you enjoy it here? Have you been eating? I hope you haven't been playing these good people up?" A flurry of questions fell from her mouth.

"Mum!" he only half complained at her attention. "I'm fine," he pushed away her hand as it wiped away an imaginary blemish of dirt from his face.

"Son," acknowledged Mr. Atwell, who remained in his seat nodding toward Dominic.

"Dad," replied Dominic, still battling with his mother's affection.

"Now Miss Hawthorne…" said Mr. Atwell sternly, "about my son."

"Yes Mr. Atwell," replied Miss Hawthorne just as curtly. "His progress at our school has been excellent, and he has proved to be a real asset to the school. You should both be proud of this young man."

Mr. Atwell seemed shocked at the news and raised an eyebrow

in surprise, "I will admit, Miss Hawthorne, that I was surprised he managed to complete the year."

"There were a couple of occasions, but on the whole boys will be boys…and his grades have improved tenfold." She took a seat behind her desk and held out a report for the parents. "As you can see, his grasp of communication has increased, while biology, geography, social, environmental and food studies have also made great leaps since his admission at Hazeldene."

"What about his maths…?" enquired Mr. Atwell.

"We are a specialized academy, Mr. Atwell, and while some programmes are catered for, others are not focused on as much."

"What is that supposed to mean?" asked Mr. Atwell.

"It means he's doing well," replied Mrs. Atwell enthusiastically. "Isn't that right?"

"Quite," agreed Miss Hawthorne.

Mr. Atwell sat for a moment in silence looking at the report in his hand, turning over the pages one at a time, studying the words written on the page. "Good enough for me," he said eventually. "Now, about next year…"

Dominic couldn't stop grinning as he sat in the back of his parent's car. Next year, he thought…I'm coming back. He had never found the prospect of school exciting, but here he was staring out of the back window at the disappearing building in the distance. He thought of his friends…Brannigan, Cooper, Penny, Dakota and, of course, Fiver…and smiled.

"Funny thing," commented Mr. Atwell as he drove up the winding road. "I know this sounds stupid, but as we were leaving I could have sworn I saw a large ape waving. You know one of those gorilla things."

Dominic sat back in his seat in the car and smiled. "Yeah dad," he smirked as he spoke. "Hilarious."

OTHER BOOKS BY THE AUTHOR

RAIN

The future is hard. Mankind has left Earth and begun its journey across the universe. A small colony has set up on a distant planet, but not everything is easy.

A colony on the brink of destruction, an ancient creature stirring from its slumber beneath the surface of the planet and storm clouds bring disaster from the skies above. As the colonists struggle to survive, a religious order attempts to bring peace between the political factions to the planet. But as the rain clouds gather, it is not just the sky which heralds death.

What is the organisation H.O.S.T and why have they come to Hope? Who really has control of the colony? What is beneath the surface, and what connection does it have with the weather system? As the tension mounts throughout the colony, the storm clouds gather overhead and with the rain...comes death.

As Rain is a sensational, thrilling and exciting, action-packed adventure that will entertain you from beginning to end, I, of course, have to award the stellar read five stars! So if you are a reader who is looking to get lost in an adventure that is thrilling as well as memorable, then Rain is for you! - Website: Red Headed Booklover Blog.

Available exclusively from Amazon.

ABOUT THE AUTHOR

*A*ndrew McDonald was born in the English city of Coventry in 1970.
From an early age, Andrew loved books and would spend hours sitting
reading and writing, creating new worlds and people. But, he never pursued a
literary career electing to leave school and seek employment rather than continue
with his studies and go to college.

In 1991, his life changed forever as he met his future wife: Mary
and together they went on to get married and have four beautiful
daughters. He would spend the next few years going from one job
to another whilst supporting his family. Along the way he never
stopped dreaming of writing and would create short stories to tell
his children to entertain them.

It would be in 2013, that his life would change and the birth of
his first granddaughter saw him make to decision to turn a past time
into a career. His love of science-fiction and in particular Doctor
Who that saw him write his first feature length title and although it
never got published, it gave him the confidence to continue.

He was commissioned to write two short stories for a Doctor
Who project in 2015 which ultimately never got published. Following these two horror stories were completed and although a
lot of interest was generated by these, neither title was published.

Despite all of this, with each rejection letter he continued believing in his dream. In 2016, he would publish his second full length story Rain through Amazon publishing and in 2018 School for Apes became his first release through an established publishing company.

Andrew McDonald still lives in Coventry with his wife and family where he writes and dreams.

Lightning Source UK Ltd.
Milton Keynes UK
UKHW040614140519
342645UK00001B/386/P